Windmill Gardens

by
Carol Ann Tardiff

ISBN 0-7414-2162-3

Cover art credit: Katie and Matthew Tardiff

Editing credit: Eleanor Burley

Quotations from:
Diary of St. Maria Faustina Kowalska, *Divine Mercy in My Soul*, copyright 1987, Congregation of Marians of the Immaculate Conception, Stockbridge, MA 01263. Used with permission.

The Holy Bible, Revised Standard Edition, copyright 1965, Thomas Nelson Publishers, Camden, NJ.

Published by:

PUBLISHING.COM

1094 New Dehaven Street, Suite 100
West Conshohocken, PA 19428-2713
Info@buybooksontheweb.com
www.buybooksontheweb.com
Toll-free (877) BUY BOOK
Local Phone (610) 941-9999
Fax (610) 941-9959

Printed in the United States of America

Printed on Recycled Paper

Published August 2004

Consecrated to:

Jesus Christ, *"My Lord, my God and my All"*
and to Mother Mary

Dedicated to:

My ever-supportive husband Dan
and our four beloved children –
Angi, Sarah, Matthew and Katie

*Note: In order to keep the continuity of the story, there are no
footnotes; however, additional information for particular chapters
is given at the end of the book.*

"I want to be completely transformed into Your mercy and to be Your living reflection, O Lord. May the greatest of all divine attributes, that of Your unfathomable mercy, pass through my heart and soul to my neighbor."

St. Maria Faustina Kowalska
Diary, #163

1

In the Woods

Desperately pushing her way through the underbrush and dodging around trees, she ran until her heart pounded as if it would burst and her breaths became hard gasps. All at once, her tortured legs buckled under her and she pitched forward onto the weed-covered dirt. Immediately she rolled over, sat up, and glanced hurriedly in all directions around her. There seemed to be nothing moving in this part of the woods, but the teenage girl continued to frantically look around her while listening intently over the raspy sound of her own labored breathing.

After a few minutes, she awkwardly shrugged the canvas pack off her back, pushed it aside and eased backward onto her elbows before dropping flat on her back on the hard ground. There she lay for quite some time, trying to catch her breath while staring up at the overhead canopy of leaves. Every so often she would lift her head and scan the area. Still there was nothing obviously alarming to be seen.

Eventually her heart rate slowed to normal and she turned with a grimace of pain onto her side. Her eyes squeezed tightly shut, she lay there quietly for a moment. But soon she buried her face into the crook of her arm and her shoulders shook with great wrenching sobs.

Much later, with dusk beginning to fall, the girl wiped her face on the sleeve of her sweatshirt and hauled herself stiffly onto her feet. Looking about, she spied a thick tangle of bushes whose arching branches formed a sheltered spot beneath. Crawling under them, she pulled her jacket over herself and rested her head on the backpack. Her eyes didn't close, though, until a long time after darkness set in.

The next morning found the girl sitting upright at the foot of a large maple, positioned so that the sun spilled out its rays over the length of her body. Her black jacket was spread over her blue-jeaned legs to absorb every bit of warmth possible. She had already been awake for awhile and had moved around some, but seemed unable to get the chill of the night out of her aching muscles. While basking in the early sun and leaning back against the tree, she tried to think about nothing except the day unfolding around her.

Sunlight flashed on the iridescent bodies of insects as they slowly lifted into the air to begin their daily rounds of whatever insects do. There had been a noticeable lull in the normal woodland sounds as the light breeze that had sprung up during the night died down and the air became still. But now the birds were awakening and talking noisily to their neighbors about plans for the day. Their darting movements as they dropped to lower and lower branches, then to the ground to snare an unsuspecting worm, finally broke through the girl's half-awake state.

She stood up and brushed off that part of the woods still clinging to her backside and legs. The little woodland creatures, she noticed, seemed to know exactly what needed doing on this beautiful morning. Particularly interesting was a little fellow who poked his brown head out from beneath the tree roots where the girl had been sitting. She smiled when the tiny animal scampered from his hole and perched on a fallen branch, and wondered if the chipmunk was surprised this morning to find his doorway blocked by a big two-legged creature. Of course, *she* might have been the surprised one if he had decided to take a nip!

The girl pulled a comb out of her pocket. She tried to bring some order to her tangled hair, removing bits of leaves and moss and finally remaking it into a high ponytail. Then she slung her backpack over one shoulder and set out through the woods.

Before long the trees began to thin out and soon the teenager saw clusters of buildings ahead of her. In spite of being desperately hungry and thirsty, she hung back in the shelter of the trees while waiting for more people to be out and about. Using a small mirror, she made herself look as presentable as possible, then took out a pencil and a piece of paper and concentrated on making a list.

Finally she headed toward a large convenience store behind a gas station, taking the precaution of approaching cautiously from the rear and hiding her backpack in a dense stand of evergreens and bushes nearby. With just a small black purse hanging from her shoulder, the girl casually entered the front door of the store and emerged a short time later carrying a bulging plastic bag. Sauntering to the rear of the building, she glanced around quickly and scrambled under the evergreens. She pulled a bottle of water from the shopping bag and drank it greedily, then unwrapped a granola bar and wolfed it down.

Resting on the brown-needled ground in her personal haven, the teenager took up a thoughtful posture. Her elbow on her knee and her chin cradled in her hand, she spent quite some time in deep thought and finally made a decision. First, she stowed in her backpack everything that was in the store bag. Next, she took a credit card out of her purse. For several minutes she turned the card over and over in her hand, staring at it and chewing on her lip. At last she tossed it into the plastic bag along with the empty water bottle and granola wrapper, and set the whole thing aside.

From her pack, she retrieved an apple which she quickly devoured and a map which she spread open on the ground. Leaning on one elbow, she spent some time perusing it, running her finger back and forth over it as if checking for something. She removed an envelope from her purse, looked intently at it and checked the map, then put both items along with her purse into her backpack.

After surreptitiously slipping the plastic bag with its contents into a trash can, it didn't take long before she had left the town behind. For the rest of the day, the girl traveled as quickly as she could through the woods in a general northerly direction. She kept her bearings by the position of the sun, and stopped only long enough to eat or drink something from her backpack. When it became too dark to see, she again found shelter in the underbrush. To an observer it might have looked almost as if she was beginning to enjoy her outdoor adventure. But that impression was not to last very long.

2

Lost!

All the next day she continued her journey, and the following morning the girl was once more seated on the ground next to a tree in the woods. This time, though, she had the map lying open on her lap and was studying it with a look of consternation on her young face.

I should have gotten there yesterday, she thought in dismay. *Or at least seen some signs I was getting closer.* Other than some dusty country roads running in the wrong direction, she had come upon little else but a few isolated houses and ever more woods and fields.

She puzzled over the map for a few more moments but, realizing the futility of gleaning much information from it, soon folded it and put it away. After all, a map is quite a useful tool, but the problem seemed to be that she didn't know where *she* was. And she was getting worried about her low supply of food and water. Trying not to succumb to tears again, she closed her eyes and leaned her head back against the trunk of the tree in order to think.

Suddenly, she was startled from her reverie by something crashing noisily through the bushes on her right. Her eyes flew open just in time to see the tail end of a large, long-haired animal obviously in pursuit of something. In a panic she scrambled quickly to her feet, her heart pounding wildly.

Wolf! she instantly thought. *I'm glad it didn't see me behind the tree!* Of course, the wolf could easily have caught her scent, but it seemed to be in quite a hurry to catch its prey. A frightened squeal, coming from an open area ahead of her, split the air and stopped abruptly.

As she stood there trembling and trying to think, it occurred to her that the wolf was in the direction she wanted to go.

Now what should I do? Go around the clearing? Just how big a circle would I need to make?

One after another, her options passed quickly through her mind, but in the end perhaps more than a little curiosity clouded her judgment. As quietly as possible and careful not to step on dead branches, the girl picked up a sturdy stick and crept up behind some bushes that hid the clearing from her sight.

There she crouched, undecided again and still frightened, wondering whether she was doing the wise thing. After all, a hungry wolf was hardly something one would want to fool around with. On the other hand, if it had just devoured a rabbit or a squirrel, it couldn't still be hungry, could it?

Finally making up her mind, she took a deep breath and held it while standing up straighter to peer over the top of the bushes. What she saw made her exhale suddenly, and a small laugh escaped in spite of her best efforts to stop it.

A wolf? Yeah, right! What made me think there'd be a wolf around here?

At the unexpected sound, the large animal, standing in the bright morning sun a dozen yards from her, dropped the limp body of a rabbit that had been dangling from its jaws and looked toward her with its ears pricked. Then it put its head down and nosed the rabbit, looked up again at the girl, wagged its tail once and bounded away from her into the woods.

A German Shepherd! And a not-very-hungry one at that!

Dropping the stick, the girl chuckled at her silly fears and walked into the open field to have a look at the rabbit. With compassion on her face, she probed the dead animal with the toe of her shoe.

Immediately an idea popped into her mind. *Food!*

Then another thought hit her. *What if the dog was out here in the woods with someone?!*

She suddenly felt exposed and nervous in the sunlight, so she quickly seized the rabbit by its ears. Holding it well away from herself, she returned to the darker shelter of the trees. She nervously looked around in all directions but saw nothing moving other than a few birds.

Dropping the animal onto a patch of grass, the girl gathered up dry leaves, twigs and a few larger sticks. Careful to clear the area of anything else that might catch fire, she piled up the kindling and took a disposable lighter out of her backpack.

Thank goodness I don't have to use flint like pioneers did! She held the flame to the curled-up, papery leaf edges.

When the fire was blazing strongly, she turned her attention to the rabbit. From the main compartment of her pack she pulled out a clear, plastic package containing…a sharp kitchen knife! For a few stressful moments, it seemed as if it might defy any attempts to extricate it from its tough packaging without the aid of scissors. It took a bit of effort, but determination at last prevailed.

The girl reflected how glad she was that she had decided, at the last minute, to add the knife to her basket of items at the store. At the time, it had seemed to her that it would be handy to have for protection. Now she wondered a bit ruefully why she had thought it would be helpful in an emergency. She felt rather foolish, picturing herself trying to use the knife, still encased in plastic, to thwart an attacker. The girl decided she had better set that troubling thought aside and begin the distasteful task of skinning the rabbit.

She grimaced as she cut off the head and the feet, slashed the skin and peeled it off, and then sliced open the body to remove the insides as best she could. *Eeugh! What a mess!* Cutting a thin but sturdy branch from a nearby tree, she stripped off the bark, speared the rabbit meat and held it over the fire until her arms ached. *Just how long does it take to cook a rabbit anyway?* she wondered.

After a long time, she was able to pull off some cooked meat. It tasted different from what she was accustomed to eating, rather bland and a little tough to chew, but it felt great to have the promise of a full stomach. Her bigger problem now was that she was dangerously low on water, as she had used some of her precious bottled water to wash the blood off her hands.

Much later that same day, in the heat of the afternoon, she came upon a stream. It was shallow and not very wide, and the green slippery bottom didn't look very inviting. Still, the girl eagerly picked her way down the stony bank. At the water's edge she set her backpack on a rock where it would stay dry, set her shoes next to it with her socks stuffed inside, rolled up her jeans as far as they would go and stepped gingerly into the water.

Aah! That feels good! she thought, watching the fine silt cloud the water around her ankles. The day had warmed up so much that the skin on her feet was tight and blistery. Once the water had settled a bit, she splashed the refreshing coolness up the calves of her legs and slid wet hands up and down her forearms. She had fine red lines lacing her arms and hands from the brambles in the woods, and the water greatly helped relieve the sting of the scratches.

Looking at the slow-moving water dividing around her legs, she briefly considered getting the empty bottles out of her pack and filling them in the stream. After all, it looked inviting and clear enough when it wasn't stirred up, and her water supply was really low. However, she decided that that might be a dumb thing to do.

Who knows what invisible germs or microbes lurk in even the cleanest-looking water? She realized the last thing she needed was to be out here in the wilderness doubled over in agony from intestinal parasites.

Then she looked down at her arms, wondering if microscopic organisms could enter the bloodstream through scratches on the skin. She frowned, wiped her arms against her T-shirt and decided against splashing any water on her perspiring face, no matter how good it might feel.

Retrieving her stuff, the girl waded to the other side of the stream and, after replacing her socks and shoes, climbed the bank to continue on her way. Discouraged and weary, she just kept putting one foot in front of the other all that afternoon.

One thing for sure, she determined to herself, *no matter what, I'm not going back.*

She tried to fortify herself for the challenges that likely lay ahead. But there was no way she could have foreseen the surprises the end of the day would bring.

3

The Garden

The blue sky was starting to cloud up around the edges, and there was a haziness in the air that hinted at rain. The day had become hot and very sticky, and so was the girl as she kept trudging through the woods. Hungry and thirsty – the morning's breakfast of rabbit meat long since digested – she had just one granola bar and very little water left. With evening coming, she began to think about looking for some heavy bushes to crawl under, in order to have some protection from the soaking that the sky was promising.

As she walked and searched for a likely spot, her mind mulled over many things. *What should I do if I see a farm in the distance?* That thought brought a grim smile to her face. She could just imagine emerging from the woods, marching up to a farmhouse and telling the occupants that she was starving to death. That might be kind of weird, but the next thoughts weren't very funny at all. What if they locked the door against this strange, unkempt girl trespassing on their land? Or worse, what if they called the police?

Trying to beat down the panicky feeling that arose in her chest, she firmly scolded herself. *I'm not that desperate yet! I can last a little longer on what I've got. And maybe I can figure out how to catch some rainwater tonight.*

At that moment, as she circled around a thicket of hedge-like bushes, the girl noticed ahead of her a small structure of some sort. She stopped as far from it as she could, puzzling over what it could be and why it was out here in what seemed to be the middle of the woods. The building was only about as wide as the spread of one's arms and maybe twice as tall. Its weathered grey wood siding looked quite dilapidated. But it was the rusty pipe on the roof, sticking up like a vent, that led her to conclude that what she had found just might be an old outhouse. She cautiously made her way around to the other side and, sure enough, on a slightly sagging wooden door with rusty hinges, was the universal sign of a cut-out crescent moon. She pulled on the latch and the door reluctantly creaked open.

The girl instinctively wrinkled her nose and held her breath. However, she found not a foul odor but only a tangle of old dusty cobwebs, which she proceeded to sweep away with a leafy branch. And when she discovered a partial roll of toilet paper hanging on its holder, she decided to take advantage of the accommodations. She was careful to check for spiders or other biting creatures that might be lurking in the vicinity. Still, compared with trying to manage in a primitive way in the woods, this was luxury indeed!

She emerged from the outhouse and it wasn't long before she came upon a footpath in the weeds. *Okay,* she decided on a whim. *I'm going to follow it. If it leads to a farm, then I'll figure out what to do.*

After a few minutes, she saw a squirrel running toward her on the trail. All of a sudden it noticed her, and the little animal in one smooth motion leaped onto a nearby tree. She hurried ahead to watch it, curious about what it had in its mouth. But the dim light made it difficult to see the squirrel as it scurried higher. She continued on the path and soon saw yet another squirrel running toward her.

This one, though, didn't see her until almost the last moment. Startled, he dropped what he was carrying, bounded up the closest tree and sat chittering at her from a branch high above her head. She bent down to retrieve what the squirrel had dropped and found some food in the palm of her hand.

Under normal circumstances what she retrieved from the ground might not be considered much of a meal. But when one is hungry and holding a peanut in its shell in one's hand, well, it doesn't take long to break it open and pop the nut into a grateful mouth. And if a couple of squirrels had managed to find such a treat for themselves, could there be more in the vicinity?

Ahead of her, in the direction from which the squirrels had come, the girl could see the brighter area of a clearing. As she went toward the light and stepped out of the woods, the setting sun broke briefly through the clouds and lit up before her a small circular meadow, covered with the white blossoms of clover. The path continued through this glowing meadow into what seemed to be a solid wall of bushes and evergreen trees on the opposite side.

Curiosity, and yet another squirrel with a peanut, were what convinced the girl to follow the trail across the clearing, approach a barely-seen narrow opening in the greenery and set her backpack down under the evergreens. The dense foliage prevented her from catching any glimpse of what was beyond. Consequently, when she crept closer and carefully poked her head around the edge of the gap, she was absolutely astounded at what lay before her eyes.

Flowers! And more flowers! Flowers upon flowers upon flowers! Clouds were quickly covering the deepening hues of the evening sky, but even in the fading light she could see a beautiful garden, a veritable landscape of colored blossoms – reds and yellows, blues, purples and especially whites, which stood out starkly in the semi-darkness, almost as if they had a particular source of illumination. The breeze, previously gentle but now beginning to take on a briskness with the impending rain, rustled through and around the sea of flowers, setting each of them dancing and bobbing as though nodding and welcoming in her direction. The wind also carried the most delightfully sweet floral perfume to her. It was this scent which brought her out of the trance that engulfed her from the first moment she set eyes on the incredible garden.

When she lifted her head and looked over the tallest flowers, she could just make out the back of a long, low house at the far end of the garden. She could see even more flowers, in pots or baskets, hanging along the edge of its roof. There was no one anywhere in the garden, and all the windows of the house were dark. In the rapidly gathering gloom, she brought her attention back to a low-edged, round pan lying not too far from her on the garden path. Near it sat a squirrel, greedily crunching a peanut held tightly in its little paws.

Stealthily the girl stepped into the garden. Forming a sort of crude pocket with the bottom edge of her shirt, she stooped down – frightening the squirrel away in the process – and quickly scooped up the remaining peanuts. Holding her T-shirt with its treasure tucked tightly against her stomach, she hurried out of the garden to where she had dropped her pack. While breaking open the shells and stuffing the nuts into her mouth, her mind busily churned over what she had seen.

That is some garden!

Although she hadn't paid much attention at the time, it seemed that there had been a small shed-like building to her right as she had entered the garden. But there was something else that she was trying to remember, too, and it suddenly came to her.

A hose! A garden hose! Now she was certain there had been a hose lying on the ground close to the squirrels' pan. *Was there any chance that the hose had been left on?*

The very thirsty girl knew she had to find out. Pulling an empty bottle out of her backpack and slinging the pack over one shoulder, she peeked once more through the gap in the bushes. There was still no one in sight. She crept to where the hose lay, put the nozzle into the neck of the bottle and pulled the trigger.

Water! Not very much, as the faucet had likely been turned off, but what was left in that long hose filled her bottle half full before slowing to a trickle, then a drip. In the next instant, water came in abundance, but not from the hose. The sky began to open up as she started to leave the garden.

Without a second thought, when she reached the door of the shed she pulled sharply on its handle. The door swung open and she quickly slipped inside. Closing it behind her against the rain, barely able to see anything in the dim light, the girl waited a moment until her eyes adjusted. Then she could make out the interior, which she had expected to be filled with junk, as sheds usually are. But this one was nearly empty, having only some pieces of wood of various lengths and shapes standing at the other end. The shed itself was quite roomy, about ten feet across and a little longer, and there were windows on the side facing the house. Peering through them, the girl was reassured that no one was coming in the downpour to kick her out.

Best of all, on the back wall of the shed opposite the windows, there was a built-in bench, topped with moth-eaten but soft cushions. Here she sat to drink her meager ration of water, and here she decided to stretch out her exhausted body until the first light of day.

4

The Gardener

The woman sat at her kitchen table in front of a large picture window, with several open books spread out before her. It was unusually dark outside for so early in the evening, but she had already noticed the heavy grey clouds rolling in. *Rain right now would be a blessing,* she thought. *This first part of June has been so dry. And even May didn't get much.*

As the natural light started to fade inside the house, she didn't bother to get up to turn on a lamp. This was her favorite time of day, if one part of the day could really be better than another. Supper and the day's chores were finished. Resting here in the deepening twilight, looking at the lovely garden just outside the window, instilled such a sense of peace within her and gratitude to God for his gracious bounty. Not that her joints didn't ache and her back wasn't tired, for a garden such as this happened only with a ton of honest, hard work. But the beauty laid out in front of her eyes made it all worthwhile. She closed every evening she could in just such a manner, enjoying the garden as it slipped into shadows and, in the last of the natural light, praying the Psalm for the Evening and reading a bit of Scripture.

As the kitchen continued to darken and it became increasingly impossible to read, the woman pushed aside the books. She sat up closer to the table with her elbows resting on it and her hands clasped out in front of her. She looked out at the flowers which were starting to sway and ripple like waves in the quickening wind, yet now she didn't really see them. The psalm and the Bible verses had merely lit the pathway to her own personal prayer, that prayer that sprang naturally to her heart and mind when she had a few quiet moments like these.

Closing her eyes, she continued to speak to the Lord as if he was sitting there at her kitchen table, listening to her and fascinated by everything she said. She didn't pray with fancy words, but simply and from the heart. She asked God questions and she thanked him over and over again. She also prayed for guidance for herself and help for all her family and friends.

Finally, she opened her eyes as the last vestige of light faded from the house. As she refocused on the garden which was still slightly brighter, she was suddenly alarmed.

There was someone in the garden!

At the far end, she saw a figure crouched down behind the squirrels' food pan. He was scooping up the peanuts that were there and stuffing them into a pocket. If it wasn't for the person's white shirt which stood out starkly in the dim light, she wasn't sure if she would have seen him at all.

Quickly she got up and made sure the outside door of the back utility room was locked, then grabbed a pair of binoculars which were hanging on a hook next to the door. Returning to the kitchen window, careful not to move the curtains, she used the binoculars to try to see the intruder a little better.

But the person, whoever it was, was gone. The woman searched the entire garden with the binoculars, then lowered them and took a deep breath to steady herself. In all her years in this house, she had never had anyone come into her backyard from the woods. Now she was feeling vulnerable living here on her own.

She continued standing there and every few minutes used the binoculars to scan the entire garden. Not much time had passed when, squinting her eyes in the gloom of twilight, she caught another flash of white. He had returned!

The binoculars enabled her to see what she could never have seen otherwise. The person was bending down and picking up the garden hose, and now stood up. She was surprised that it didn't seem to be a man, after all, but a girl with a ponytail and a backpack.

She also noticed that rain was beginning to fall, and saw the girl open the door to the workshop and disappear inside. The woman sank down slowly into her chair and stayed there for quite a while, chin in the palm of her hand, deep in thought.

At least she'll be dry, and the poor thing didn't look too threatening. But why would a young girl be out here in the middle of nowhere by herself? And how could she be so hungry and thirsty that she'd resort to taking peanuts from squirrels and trying to get water from a hose?

13

5

Fire!

The next morning, as was customary for her, the woman was again seated at her table in the kitchen. The same books were open before her, only now there was·a cup of herbal tea steaming next to them. She was up a little earlier than usual because she had not slept well, waking up now and again to wonder about and pray for the young person outside. By rising before dawn she hoped to catch another glimpse. And it wasn't long before she saw the workshop door open and the girl, without a backward glance, disappear through the hedge.

Well, maybe that was that, she thought.

But whether or not she ever saw the girl again didn't stop the woman from praying for her. She was very concerned, because the sky was still quite overcast and it was likely this new day would bring more showers.

Whatever is that child going to do if it pours? And even if it doesn't rain, her clothes and shoes are going to get soaked in the woods. It's so chilly at night, even now in June. That poor child – wherever could she have come from?

As she started her day's work, she worried and prayed for the girl. She prepared herself some breakfast and worried where the girl was going to get food. She donned a light jacket before venturing out into the damp backyard and worried how the girl would stay warm in only a short-sleeved shirt. As she pulled the weeds, which detached easily from the garden's sodden soil, she prayed for the children who always seemed to bear the brunt of the world's troubles. Straightening some of the taller plants that had hunched over against last night's shower, she worried whether the authorities should be notified.

However, this last she decided against. She would wait for awhile and see where this would lead. Anyway, there was a *lot* of woods in the area that would have to be searched.

A light drizzle eventually drove the woman inside where, as she worked on her household chores, she finally left the problem in God's hands. There wasn't much she could do about it anyway. But late in the afternoon as the sky began to clear, it suddenly occurred to her that she could put out a little sustenance for the girl in the slim chance she might return.

She looked around the kitchen, trying to decide what she might put in the squirrels' pan. Apples? No, that might look too obvious. She didn't want to scare the child away. Some bread? People put out bread for squirrels all the time. However, if it rained, it would turn to mush. In the end, she opted for peanuts again. And perhaps twice the usual amount would be a good idea.

She brought the big round pan in the house and gave it a good scrubbing, dried it well and returned it to the end of the garden, heaped high with its offering of peanuts in their protective shells. Then she thought of the long hose lying nearby on the ground, and had the inspiration to make sure the nozzle end was turned off and the faucet end was turned on. That way it would look as if she had just forgotten about it when she had finished her chores for the day.

Once more the woman was at her table as evening approached. When she had prepared supper earlier, she had stayed away from the large window so she couldn't be seen. Now with her prayer books in front of her and the binoculars close at hand, she watched and waited and prayed. Dusk had only begun when she saw the slight figure of the girl again appear, first hesitating in the hedge gap, then quickly moving to the hose to fill a bottle and then to the squirrel's pan, where she dumped the peanuts into her backpack.

This time the girl had on a dark long-sleeved top. But since it was lighter outside tonight, the woman, even without the help of the binoculars, was able to see her clearly. She noticed how quickly the girl opened the door to the workshop and slipped inside, and she thanked God that the child had taken advantage of the shelter once again. There had been hardly a hint of sun all day and the night would certainly be cool.

Lord, should I be doing something more for that child? But she could see me through the front windows and take off before I get there. Perhaps, she thought, *I should write a note offering to help and tape it to the workshop door after dark tonight.* For a long time as the light continued to fade, the woman prayed for guidance.

Suddenly, from behind her, came a sharp knock on the front door. She jumped at the sound, but was unable to push her chair back before the doorknob turned and a dark-haired head poked inside.

"Del, are you here?" a deep voice called.

"Oh, Richard, it's you! Come on in."

The woman stood up and was turning around when a tall, broad-shouldered man came through the doorway of the kitchen. He was dressed in old blue jeans and a worn, grubby shirt, and there was a wide smile on his friendly-looking face.

"Now, Del, haven't I told you before about keepin' your doors locked, especially when it's gettin' dark? I mean, just think about who might walk in!" the man said, with a little twinkle in his eye. On the counter he set a quart jar and a cardboard egg carton.

"Here's your milk 'n eggs. You told me you had enough cream to last you for awhile. And I brought those bales of straw you wanted. They're in the truck. I'll drop 'em out back for you."

Richard was talking so much he didn't even notice that his friend seemed rather distracted. As he started to launch into a story about one of his kids, he happened to glance through the big window at the garden outside. He suddenly stopped mid-sentence and his mouth dropped open.

"Del!" he shouted. "The workshop is on fire!!"

The woman spun around quickly and looked outside. Sure enough, even in the twilight one could see smoke curling from the cracks around the door of the workshop. She bolted to the back door, flung it open and was running down the main garden path before Richard realized what was happening. He took off after her and his long legs quickly caught him up to her. Laying hold of her arm, he yelled, "Del, don't! It's not worth getting hurt for an empty building!"

But Del didn't stop. She pulled away and tried to run even faster. "There's someone in there!" she gasped, her face showing how upset she was.

Someone was in the workshop?

Surprise made Richard slow momentarily before he quickened his stride and ran past Del. He noticed the hose lying on the ground, snatched it up and pulled the trigger on the nozzle just as he reached the door and flung it open. Smoke poured out but he immediately trained the water stream on some smoldering material he saw on the floor. Realizing that the source of the problem was an old space heater, he yanked its plug from the outlet.

Del was right behind him and pushed past him to get inside. Squinting in the semi-darkness and waving the smoke away, she first checked the bench along the back wall. But there was only a dirty backpack. Meanwhile, Richard flipped on the light switch and, in the dim light from the overhead bulb, hurried to the other end of the workshop.

"Del, there's someone here on the floor!"

Together the two of them turned over the still form.

"Why, it's a young girl!" the man exclaimed in a puzzled voice. Del examined her more closely and determined that she was breathing. So Richard carefully gathered the girl in his arms and carried her out of the workshop, where the onslaught of cool evening air revived her momentarily. Seeing a man's face looming over her and feeling his arms around her, she seemed to panic and began to beat at him with her fists. But Richard was strong and held on tightly. In a second or so, she went limp again and he carried her through the back door and kitchen, into the living room.

Del, trotting as fast as she could after him, turned on some lamps in the room and instructed, "Put her there on the couch."

Richard laid his burden down gently and, looking more closely at the girl, said, "She's breathin' okay. I'll bet she just fainted. Tell you what. I'm gonna run home and send Ann back to take a look at her."

He sprinted out the front door. Del was left standing there in her own living room, looking down at a teenage girl *(fifteen maybe?)* with dirty blond hair pulled back from her thin face, muddy, torn clothing and only a filthy pair of socks on her feet.

Okay, Lord, I wanted to help. What do I do now?

6

House of Books

When the girl came to, she saw an attractive woman who was perhaps in her thirties sitting next to her. The woman was holding her right hand and patting it gently. When she saw the girl's eyes open, she smiled and said, "Hi! How are you feeling?"

Cautiously, the girl studied her for a moment. She saw a heart-shaped face that was framed by softly-waved auburn hair, and a pair of sparkling grey-blue eyes. The eyebrows were raised like question marks. Around the woman's neck was a stethoscope hanging over a pretty flowered blouse.

"Okay, I guess," replied the girl in a low voice, then turned her head toward the sound of someone else entering the room. Into view came another woman carrying the girl's backpack and shoes, with a long flashlight tucked under her arm. The woman set the items down on the floor and came over to the sofa.

This woman was really old – *at least fifty,* the teenager decided – with straight hair that probably had been jet black when she was younger, but was now streaked with grey and pulled back into a bun behind her neck. Her face was slightly rounded as was the rest of her. Behind a pair of small, rimless glasses were warm brown eyes that crinkled around the edges when she smiled, like she was doing now.

The younger woman glanced up at the new arrival, saying, "Well, she doesn't seem to be any worse for wear. At first I was afraid of smoke inhalation, but I think Richard was right – she just fainted. She has a small abrasion on her forehead but doesn't seem to have a concussion. The biggest problem is she's dehydrated and looks like she hasn't had a square meal for awhile."

The woman who was talking looked back at the girl and apologized.

"I'm sorry, sweetie, I haven't introduced myself. My name is Ann. I'm a registered nurse. You're sure you feel okay?"

She stopped, perhaps waiting for a return introduction, but the girl just nodded and remained silent.

The one who was a nurse stood up and both women walked to the front door. As they stepped outside and carried on a discussion in low tones – *sounds like they disagree on something,* she thought – the girl glanced around at the house itself. The living room where she was lying on a sofa was softly lit. She could look through a wide doorway straight ahead into the kitchen, where there was a table in front of a large, night-blackened picture window. Past her stockinged feet, which looked pretty gross to her at the moment, were two closed doors. *Probably bedrooms,* she decided, and when she twisted her neck to look behind her she could see a couple more doors which were open.

The wood floor in the living room was covered with a multi-patterned fringed rug, giving the room a comfortable, homey feel. There wasn't much on the walls except a cross next to the kitchen doorway. Most of the wall space was taken up by bookshelves. There were tall bookshelves and shorter ones and, if there was one thing this place didn't lack, it was books. There were books on the shelves and books on top of the bookcases. More books were lying on the end table and piled on the floor next to a stuffed easy chair. *Do all these books mean that a family lives here? It doesn't seem like a very large house.*

By now the older woman had returned and gone into the kitchen, calling back over her shoulder, "Ann says getting water into you is the first order of business."

After bringing a glass of water, she helped the girl into a sitting position.

"Easy now, don't sit up too fast. And drink it slowly," she ordered, although she was smiling as she said it.

While the girl gratefully drank the water, the woman returned to the kitchen to warm up some food.

"I hope you like soup," she called. "And," muttering almost to herself, "maybe I can find some crackers around here."

Right about now the girl would have eaten dog food if it was offered to her, but soup sounded a lot more pleasant. As she quickly finished the bowl of soup, the woman didn't say a word, but just went to get a refill. Then she dragged in a kitchen chair, pulled it up in front of the sofa and plopped herself down to watch the girl eat.

19

7

Lucky Girl

With compassion, the woman noticed the teenage girl trying hard not to wolf down the food. Finally, praying for the right words to say, she broke the silence.

"My name is Del," she said, then stopped, hoping for a reply. But the girl just concentrated on tipping the bowl up to her mouth to get the last drops.

"I'll be glad to bring you some more, but maybe we'd better let those two bowls settle a bit first." Del went on, leaning forward a little with concern in her face, "You know, you're a pretty lucky child not to have died from all that smoke."

At that, the girl looked at the woman with eyes that seemed – what? Cautious? Frightened? She answered Del in a low voice, "Thank you for rescuing me." She dropped her gaze and added, "I'm sorry for burning up your shed."

The woman chuckled. "Burning up? Hardly! There was just a lot of smoke and it's all cleared out. Thank goodness the floor is concrete or it might've been a different story. I think some mice had gotten in and made their nest from straw and dry grass underneath that old space heater. I haven't been in there for years. It was my husband's workshop. I'm just glad you found a place out of the rain."

The young girl seemed genuinely sorry as she explained, "I was so cold. My clothes and shoes were wet, so when I noticed the heater there, I thought I'd turn it on just long enough to warm up. But I was so tired I fell asleep, and when I woke up the whole place was filled with smoke."

She paused to take a breath and Del waited patiently.

"I was afraid to go past the heater to get to the door. So I went to the other end to find a window or something. But I guess I must've hit my head on the wood there." She rubbed her head. "I don't remember anything else…"

She stopped abruptly and a sudden look of fright came into her face. "But there was a man…"

Del cut in quickly, "That was just Richard, my neighbor. Ann's husband. He was the one who first noticed the smoke and put the fire out with the hose…Why, child," she said, her eyes opening wider, "God must really be watching over you. I left that hose on so you could get a drink and we were darned lucky to have it when we needed it!"

The girl looked down at her lap and didn't say anything else. So Del, never one to let the conversation lag too long, continued, "I live here by myself, so you don't need to be frightened. There's no one else around. Richard and Ann Spencer live on a farm down the road a piece with their two children…Well, soon to be three! Did you notice? Ann has a baby on the way!"

Del smiled broadly. But it didn't seem like the girl was much interested in anyone else as she asked, "So you knew I was in the shed…uh, workshop, last night?"

Del's eyes twinkled as she nodded.

"Why did you think there were so many peanuts out there tonight?"

She stopped, noticing how exhausted the girl looked.

"Say, how would you like to take a shower?"

The girl brightened considerably.

"Tell you what. I'm going to dig through my stuff for something you can wear. When you take your clothes off, just set them outside the bathroom door. I'll throw them in the washing machine so they'll be ready for you in the morning. But first, why don't you clean out your backpack so I can dry that for you too?"

Del went to the kitchen to get a paper bag for the girl to put her stuff in. When she saw the empty wrappers and plastic bottles being pulled from the pack, she went to fetch the wastebasket, too. After the trash came a folded map which was a little damp, a disposable lighter, a comb, a knife – *Why in the world does she have a kitchen knife in her backpack?* Del wondered – and a lightweight black jacket. There was also a small purse, and the last thing to be removed from a zippered side pocket was a white envelope with the top torn open. These final two items the girl held onto, putting everything else into either the paper bag or the wastebasket.

Del got some clothes from her bedroom, gave them to the girl and showed her where the bathroom was. When dirty clothing appeared outside the bathroom door, she picked the items up rather gingerly and dropped them into the washer. Next she took the backpack and the girl's tennis shoes and hung them in the back room to dry. She checked the bed in the guest room to make sure there were clean sheets on it, set out a plate of biscuits and a glass of milk on the bedside table, then sat down in the living room to collect her thoughts and talk over the evening's events with the Lord.

She had plenty of opportunity to do so, as the girl spent quite a long time in the bathroom. *It must feel pretty good after roughing it,* smiled Del to herself. *I wonder how long it's been since she's had a shower. From the condition, and smell, of her clothes I'd guess it's been a while.*

From thinking to praying and back again, Del's head began to slowly lean back against the chair cushion and her eyes closed. She only snapped awake when the bathroom door opened.

As the girl walked into the living room, Del took one look at her and clapped her hand over her mouth. She tried not to laugh, but her round face crumpled up, her eyes crinkled and a small snort escaped from her nose.

I guess her wearing my clothes is not going to work!

She suppressed a grin as she surveyed the overly-wide shirt and the bottom of the too-short pants floating somewhere around mid-calf on the girl, who was much taller than she. It even brought a smile to the girl's face as she looked down at herself, scrunching together the extra fabric in the waist area and holding it against her gaunt body.

"Well!" said Del at last. "At least the socks fit."

They both burst out laughing, and it was a good way to end the stressful evening. Del found a roomy nightgown for her guest and showed her to the bedroom. After that she locked up the house for the night, turned out the lights and retired to her own room to lay the day's concerns at the feet of her Lord.

8

Morning

Del knelt at the edge of one of the smaller garden plots in her backyard, pulling the weeds that had popped up despite her best efforts at mulching with straw. But after a few moments she sat back on her heels, reflecting on the events of the previous evening and on the strange girl who was still asleep in the guest bedroom. Del had been up not long after the sun rose, first tossing the wet clothes from the washer into the dryer, then drinking her ritual cup of tea at the kitchen table while her morning prayers tumbled from her heart.

Now, stretching a bit to relieve her stiff joints, she basked in the warm sun which felt so good after the damp, cool night. She admired the Dahlberg daisies with their vibrant yellow flowers and ferny foliage. They contrasted nicely with the taller blue bachelor's buttons in the back of the garden and the leathery leaves of the bergenia set in front. Del enjoyed the play of sunlight across the delightful textures and colors of the plants, and knew that her entire garden could be breathtaking when seen as a whole. She wondered what went through the girl's mind when she had first wandered into this paradise of flowers. As she went back to her weeding, she prayed for wisdom for the unfolding day.

Lord, what do I say to her? If I ask questions, will that scare her away?

But no answer came to mind, so Del simply prayed for the light to be guided to the next step that needed to be taken. There she left it in God's hands.

It was barely midmorning when she returned to the house. Her guest was finally awake and in the bathroom, so Del folded the clean clothes and left them outside the bathroom door. She fed the cat and set about mixing up some pancake batter. She was getting ready to pour it on the griddle when the girl entered the kitchen.

"Good morning!" Del exclaimed with a warm smile, her eyes welcoming. "Did you sleep well?"

The girl nodded and Del indicated that she should be seated at the table while the pancakes were cooking. The woman poured a glass of milk, setting it on the table along with plates and forks and a dish of butter. She noticed her guest staring out the window at the garden glowing brilliantly in the morning sunshine.

"What do you think of the garden?" she inquired.

The girl said nothing for a moment, then turning her head slowly toward Del standing by the stove, she stated simply, "I've never seen anything like it before."

The woman laughed, replying, "No, I don't suppose too many people have." She carried a platter of steaming pancakes, along with a pint-sized jar of syrup, to the table. "Help yourself. There's plenty to go around."

The girl took her at her word, heaping up several large pancakes and smothering them with butter and syrup. After the first few bites she stopped and shyly thanked Del, then asked, "What kind of syrup is this? I thought it was maple but it tastes a little different."

Del held up the glass jar and swirled around the light amber syrup inside.

"It's certainly maple, but it's from silver maple trees instead of the sugar maples which are usually used for making syrup. I made it myself."

The girl stopped eating, her fork halfway to her mouth, and repeated, "You made it yourself?"

Del chuckled at the surprised look on the girl's face.

"You bet. In late February or early March when the sap starts rising in the trees, I go out along the road where there's dozens of silver maples and drill holes in them. I tap in the spiles – you know, those little tubes that the sap drips out of? – and collect the sap in buckets. At that point the sap looks a lot like water. The buckets I put in a little wagon, or if it's too snowy I use a sled. Then I bring them home and make the syrup."

"But I remember when I was younger seeing how maple syrup was made, and you have to boil it for hours and hours and there's all that steam!"

Del's eyes crinkled, and she got a big smile on her face as she replied, "Well, that's true. You usually do. But I discovered a secret years ago about maple sap. I found that if you freeze it in plastic gallon milk jugs, then defrost the jugs about halfway, the sugary part of the sap defrosts first. So you pour that off and refreeze it. You do that twice more, and each time the sap becomes more concentrated. I end up with only a couple gallons of sap to boil down. It doesn't make a whole lot, but the taste of the syrup is worth it. Don't you agree?"

Her guest did seem to agree by how quickly she shoveled the pancakes into her mouth. She didn't even look up when the woman said, "And if you think *this* is good, you should taste birch tree syrup!"

While they ate breakfast, Del secretly studied the teenager seated diagonally across the table from her. The girl's dark-blond hair was quite straight, and pulled back into a ponytail it only accentuated the thinness of her face. The girl usually kept her gaze down, but when she did look up her blue eyes were guarded and deep shadows were beneath them.

The woman sighed a little to herself, remembering the previous evening when Ann, her neighbor, had expressed concern over Del having a stranger in her house. *If she only knew,* thought Del, *that this poor child is already in my heart.*

But all she said as they finished eating was, "How would you like a tour of the garden?"

9

Windmill

Through what Del called the "back room", where a quick stop was made so she could put on her shoes, the girl followed the woman outside onto a small flagstone patio along the back of the house. At the end of the patio, past the kitchen's large window, was a dark green metal table with several chairs around it. Along the low edge of the roof were hanging planters of all shapes and descriptions, filled with trailing vines and lovely flowers in a riot of color. There were potted plants sitting everywhere, and the girl stepped around them onto the path.

From what she could see, this wood-chipped path, about four feet wide, ran in a curving line for the entire length of the garden and ended at the workshop. Branching off from the main path were narrower walkways going off between beds of flowers, like little streams of brownish water separating from a meandering creek. Immediately to her right and left were raised beds, framed on all sides by lumber.

"These here are my vegetable gardens," Del pointed out, quite unnecessarily, as anyone could see the lettuce and cabbages and broccoli, along with the still-short vines of what might be cucumbers or squash. Even here, marigolds and other plants with bright yellow and deep red flowers were mingled in. "Companion plants," Del called them, and they gave an air of festivity even to the ordinariness of the vegetable plot.

As the woman pointed out this plant or that, the girl looked further over to her right and suddenly stopped listening. Her eyes widened as her gaze traveled upward into the blue sky. For there, behind the garage at the side of Del's garden, just past the growing vegetables, stood a tremendously tall windmill with its blades at the top catching the rays of the late morning sun.

This was not the kind of windmill that one might associate with Holland – those brown-shingled structures that look roomy enough for a windmill-keeper to dwell in, with enormous blades turning slowly in the wind. No, this one resembled a tall steel spider. Its four rust-brown spindly legs were implanted in a concrete base and its tiny body, high in the air, consisted of a circle of small blades. One larger blade-like appendage stuck out of the circle like a flag.

Well, that's weird, she thought. *Why didn't I notice this huge thing when I first came to the garden? Was I so surprised by the flowers I didn't even see it? Or was I too hungry to notice?*

She brought her eyes back to earth and turned to Del, expressing her surprise. Del pointed out that the steel of the windmill was dark-colored, and that it was twilight when the girl first came to the garden.

She continued, "That windmill has been here since the late 1800's. It was used to pump water for the farm that used to be on this land. Most of the farmland has been sold off and the original farmhouse burned down a long time ago. This house was built to replace it." She stopped for a moment, gazing up at the top of the windmill.

"When my husband and I looked into buying this place many years ago, we were fascinated by the windmill. That and the big window in the kitchen!" she said, her dark eyes sparkling.

"Was the garden here when you bought the house?" the girl asked.

"Some of it was. Over the years I just kept adding to it. My husband helped by digging the beds and hauling in wood chips. He used to tease me about 'my obsession'," Del said with a wide grin, "but he admitted that he liked not having to mow the back lawn!"

The girl looked up again at the giant windmill towering over the backyard.

"Does it still work?"

Del pointed to the top of the structure.

"See that wooden stick-like thing hanging down from the center? It's rotted now, but that used to attach to the pump down here," and she indicated an old cast-iron water pump in the center of the concrete slab base. "The wind would turn the blades and that piece would go up and down to pump the water. But, no, it didn't work even when we moved here. We have an electric pump. That old hand pump will still bring up water, though," she laughed, "if you have the perseverance – and muscle power – to work that handle!"

After that they continued their tour of the garden. Del identified the various flowers and explained how she had set up the garden plots according to the plants' watering needs.

"For instance," she gestured towards a large area at the left, "that tall plant back there, called a 'broom,' doesn't mind dry soil. It's already blossomed this spring, so I've teamed it up with later-blooming flowers, like that red coreopsis and the black-eyed Susans, because they don't need much water either. Now, you wouldn't want to plant little blue forget-me-nots here, because they like their feet wet!"

As Del focused on specific flowers and pointed out their virtues, the girl gazed out over the expanse of the extensive garden. Just as when she had had her first glimpse of it, she was struck by its astounding beauty and waves of vibrant color. Yet, now that she was up close, she could see that there were still a lot of plants that had yet to bloom this year, and there were some that had already put their best efforts forward. These dying blossoms Del pinched off as she talked, explaining that the garden was always changing throughout the growing season as the flowering plants followed through on God's perfect design for them.

The girl listened, but not very attentively. Pushing out of her mind, at least for the moment, any worries about her situation, she just let the peacefulness of the garden wash over her. That's why she was startled a bit when the woman suddenly exclaimed in a loud voice, "Oh, my gosh! It's way past lunchtime and you must be starved! Let's go in!"

10

A Surprise Under the Table

The two were just finishing their lunch, when suddenly the girl jumped a little.

"What was *that?*" she exclaimed, and pushed back her chair to peer beneath the table.

Del smiled, saying, "That must be Mama Cat. Was she rubbing against your legs?" She leaned over and spied the cat sitting there leisurely licking a paw on all sides, looking mighty pleased with herself.

"Hello, Mama. You gave our guest a bit of a scare. Come over here." She wiggled her fingers until the cat moseyed over to get a little scratch between the ears.

"A kitten!" squealed the girl, still looking under the table. Sure enough, up against the window wall where there was a corrugated box with a hole cut in front, one could see the fuzzy front paws and curious face of a tiny kitten hanging over the edge.

"Yep, Mama Cat has kittens," said Del still petting and scratching the cat. "This crazy cat showed up at my door this spring. I really had no intention of taking her in. I checked with the farms in the area to see if it was one of their barn cats, but no one recognized her. Or at least they wouldn't admit it." She smiled again.

"And how did this cat repay me for my hospitality? By presenting me with kittens! Three of them, to be exact." She bent down further and quietly scolded the mother cat who had returned to the box to lick the face of her little one.

"Would I have taken you in if I'd known you were pregnant?" But as she wagged her finger at the cat, Del had a smile on her lips and a softness in her eyes behind her round glasses.

"Do they have names?" asked the girl, sitting back up.

Del shook her head.

"Would you like to name them? There's the gold one that you can see, and there's also one that's nearly all black and one that's black and white. What do you think we should call them?"

The girl thought for a moment.

"I like the name Ginger for the gold one. The black one could be Pepper. Does the black and white one have a lot of white?"

"A fair amount."

"Well," the girl said, furrowing her brow, "I can't think of anything right now. Maybe something will come to me later."

She bent her head toward the table, and some of the hair that had come loose from her ponytail screened her face as she said softly to Del, "My name's Ariel."

Because she was looking down, the girl didn't see the look of surprise that crossed the woman's face. But Del simply said, "Well, it's nice to meet you, Ariel."

Laying her hand on the girl's arm, she continued in a compassionate voice, "Child, I don't know what kind of troubles you have. But, if you want to, you can stay here for awhile 'til you regain your strength. You could help me in the garden. There's always so much to do!"

The girl glanced up at Del's face, nodded and bit her lip before replying, "Thanks. I'd like that."

They cleaned up the dishes and went into the living room. By now it was mid-afternoon and the June sun was beating down relentlessly. Del closed the windows against the heat and pulled the shades, then turned on some fans to circulate the air.

"Sorry," she said brightly, "no air-conditioning!" She flopped down in the easy chair and picked up a rosary lying nearby on a small table. "It's too hot to do any work at this time of the day, so I usually spend an hour or so praying. Just make yourself at home. Do you like books?"

Del didn't wait for a reply, but chuckled, saying, "'Cause I sure have a lot of them! Go ahead and look at anything you want."

She closed her eyes and leaned her head back against the chair.

The girl spent some time perusing the bookshelves and the books that were piled everywhere. What an eclectic mix! There were books and magazines about gardens, but there were also many on religion. Birds, butterflies and other wildlife were the subjects of yet others, and quite a few were about herbal medicine.

On closer inspection she realized that some of what she had originally thought were magazines were, instead, catalogs. There seemed to be catalogs of every conceivable kind, but the majority were for gardening supplies.

No surprise there, she thought, picking out a handful of interesting topics from the reading material and sitting on the floor next to the sofa. She smiled to herself as a soft snore emanated from the direction of the easy chair.

Praying, huh?

But it wasn't long before she, too, rested her head on her arm outstretched on the sofa cushion and drifted into an uneasy sleep. She was only startled back into consciousness when Del jumped out of her chair, proclaiming loudly, "Heavens! Where'd the time go? We have to get going!"

11

Wilding

Get going? Go where?! The girl lumbered slowly to her feet, her mind still foggy from dozing off. The nap didn't seem to affect Del in similar manner, as she was now in the kitchen energetically packing some things into an ancient green backpack.

The woman grabbed the pack, went through the back room and was out the door before the girl was fully awake. She ran after Del and finally caught up with her halfway down the garden path.

"Where are we going?" she asked a little breathlessly.

"Wilding!" called Del over her shoulder, hurrying along.

Wilding? But there was no chance to ask further questions as Del sailed through the gap in the back hedge and into the open field that the girl recognized from before. Here Del stopped suddenly and looked around the meadow.

"How do you like my clover?" she asked. "I sowed it here, hoping that the rabbits and groundhogs would feast on it and stay out of my garden! Usually it works, but once in awhile a critter gets in and causes havoc. I feed the squirrels those peanuts for the same reason." She stopped talking and grinned. "It seems to work most of the time."

By now the girl had caught her breath. "What are you talking about?! And what do you mean by 'wilding'?"

Del said contritely, "Sorry. It's later in the day than I usually go out, so I was anxious to get to it." She explained, "In the later afternoon when it isn't as hot, I go out into the woods and fields to gather food for supper. There's *tons* of food growing wild for the taking." She swept her right arm in a wide arc. "I call it God's supermarket!"

The look on the girl's face was priceless. "You eat *weeds?*"

Del laughed, a hearty booming laugh that sprang up from deep inside. "Just follow me," she instructed.

The girl recognized the trail they were on for a short way into the woods, and then they veered off in a different direction from which she had originally come. They walked and walked as Del mentioned the various kinds of trees and the bounty they provided.

"See that shagbark hickory? And over there some oaks? They all provide nuts in the fall. The acorns, though, you'd want to boil until the tannin leaches out, or they're awfully bitter. Ones from white oaks are best, if you can keep the squirrels from hoarding them all."

They soon came out of the woods into a large clearing, where Del leaned down and pointed out the leaves of the low-growing wild strawberries. It was a large patch, which she said had provided her with a multitude of tiny, sweet red berries just recently. There were also the familiar yellow flowers of dandelions spread heavily throughout the meadow, but Del bypassed them, saying that dandelion greens were best in the spring. They followed a narrow footpath toward some high bushes and came upon a stream, merrily wending its way between banks covered with tall grasses and weeds.

Del pointed to some tall, narrow-leaved plants standing straight up along the edges of the stream, and the girl easily identified cattails. But she was surprised to learn how valuable a food source they were, from the underwater rhizomes gathered in late winter to the new shoots in spring. And the immature flower heads could be boiled like corn-on-the-cob! At this moment, though, the cattails were flowering. Del took a small paper bag out of her pack, held it up to the cattails and tapped a considerable quantity of golden pollen into it.

"What are you going to do with that?" she was asked, so she explained that the pollen was chock full of vitamins and enzymes and could be added to muffin or pancake batter.

"Do you know how much people pay at health food stores to buy little capsules of bee pollen?" Del asked. "This is all free!"

Heading away from the stream and nearing the woods again, Del showed the girl a large patch of plants about a foot-and-a-half high with toothed, pointed leaves.

"Jerusalem artichokes!" she said. "But you have to wait until the winter or early spring to dig up their edible tubers. You can buy powdered Jerusalem artichoke root at health food stores, but it costs an arm and a leg."

Del stopped before re-entering the woods, took a small hand shovel out of her pack and began to dig in the soil around a low plant that had giant, coarse leaves with wavy edges.

"Lucky it rained recently," she panted, as she worked hard to scrape the dirt away from what looked like a very large root, deeply embedded in the ground. "This is burdock. Do you know how much...?"

"...this sells for at a health food store?" The girl finished the sentence for her, and Del chuckled as she gave the root a final twist and yanked it out. She knocked as much soil off the root as she could and stowed it, stripped of leaves, in her backpack.

"You can use only the first-year plants. The second year it sends up a flower stalk and the root becomes too tough to eat."

On the way back through the meadow leading into her garden, Del knelt down and pulled up a small plant with clover-like leaves and exquisite yellow flowers.

"Wood sorrel," she said. "Here, try some," and she pulled off a small bunch of leaves to hand over.

At first the girl was hesitant, but she seemed pleasantly surprised as she gingerly bit off a piece.

"It's kind of lemony!" she exclaimed, and Del agreed.

Back in the house, the woman set about peeling and grating the burdock root, then put it in a pan with a little water to simmer. While she diced onions and shredded a carrot and mixed them into ground beef for the main dish, she had the girl set the table and put out some bread and butter. Del mixed the cooked burdock with the meat and vegetables and some seasonings, formed the mixture into patties and set them to fry in a skillet.

"Here's some lettuce to tear up into that wooden bowl there. Then you can take the wood sorrel we picked, pull off the leaves and put those in the salad, too," she instructed.

The girl did as she was asked. As the little leaflets drifted down into the bowl she exclaimed, "They're *hearts!*"

Del laughed. Indeed, the leaves did look like little green hearts, lying delicately on top of the salad.

"Isn't it something," she said, smiling, "how God can speak of his love for us in the most ordinary things?"

12

From Here to There

The next morning when Del came back into the house after her garden chores, she found the girl already up and dressed. Del took one look at her and, frowning, exclaimed, "Oh, my goodness! We can't have you keep wearing those same clothes every day!"

She paused.

"And it's obvious you can't wear mine."

That brought a smile to both their faces. Then Del was struck by a thought.

"Wait here a minute."

Del went swiftly to the other bedroom door that, up to now, had remained closed. She shut it behind her and the girl could hear drawers being pulled open. In a moment the woman emerged with some jeans and shirts thrown over her arm.

"Here we go!" she said. "When my youngest son went to college he left a lot of stuff behind. In all these years he's never bothered to take everything with him. He's thin, like you, though a bit taller. Here, try these on."

As it turned out, the clothes did fit the girl quite well. She just had to roll up the bottòms of the pants a little. When Del realized that the waist was a trifle large, she returned to the bedroom and rummaged up a belt.

Once they had settled the clothing problem, Del decided to scramble some eggs for breakfast. She asked the girl to get the egg carton out of the refrigerator, and smiled when the teenager said, amazement in her voice, "What *are* these? Easter eggs?!"

The opened carton showed eggs in muted shades of tan and pale green and even peach.

"Oh, they're from Richard's farm," Del replied. "Actually Ann and the boy take care of the chickens. They have unusual kinds of chickens and they lay unusual eggs. They taste the same, though!"

The girl shrugged and set about breaking the eggs into a bowl. *She didn't say much about last night's supper,* Del thought to herself, *and now she's going to think breakfast is a bit strange! But more importantly, what do I do about her? There must be someone frantic about her disappearance. Should I try asking a few questions?*

However, Del just felt a quietness in her spirit and a gentle invitation to keep trusting and leave each moment to God. So as they ate, she talked about the garden and what needed to be done that day. It was only as they were finishing their breakfast that she said something that caused an unanticipated reaction from the girl. Del threw out the casual remark that the day ahead was going to be quite hot, even though the morning had been chilly – but what else could you expect here in Michigan? At that, she heard a sharp intake of breath and she looked up to see the girl's eyes wide open and staring strangely.

"Michigan?!" The single word sounded a bit strangled.

Del was puzzled.

"Of course, child. Where did you think you were?"

There was no reply. A couple of tears welled up in blue eyes and trickled down an ashen face. The girl looked down and Del waited quietly. A few minutes passed and it seemed like there was nothing else forthcoming, so Del finally broke the silence with a gentle question.

"Honey, can I ask where it is you are going?"

At first there was no answer. Perhaps the girl was trying to figure out whether to trust the woman. Finally, in a low voice, she named a city in Ohio.

Del was astonished, replying, "But child, that's several hours' drive south of here!" The girl bent her head further over her plate and more tears began, soundlessly, to fall.

Del went to get the girl a tissue, then rummaged through a drawer in the living room and brought back a map. Pushing aside the breakfast dishes, she spread it open on the table and said, "Let's take a look at this. Maybe I can help you in some way."

The distraught teenager wiped her eyes and looked at the map. Hesitantly, and without revealing from where she had initially started out, she ran a finger up the western side of Ohio.

"There was this man," she said in a tremulous voice, "who offered to give me a ride up this highway here. He was kinda old and seemed nice enough, so I didn't worry too much at first. He talked a lot in the beginning, but after awhile he got quieter and quieter. I tried asking him how far he was going, but he wouldn't answer. He kept driving and driving and wouldn't respond to any of my questions. Then he turned off the highway onto a side road, and I started getting really scared. So I told him I needed to use the john, and he stopped at a gas station."

She paused for a moment to take a deep breath. Del said nothing, waiting for the girl to continue.

"I climbed out the bathroom window, and found myself at the edge of a woods, so I took off. I ran as far as I could through the woods. When I was too tired to run anymore, I found a place under some bushes to spend the night. The next morning I walked 'til I came to a town where I bought some supplies. And a map, like this one," she indicated with her hand.

"So I looked at the map and figured out I needed to go directly north to get to the city where my dad lives."

She stopped abruptly and nervously bit a fingernail. It was obvious to Del that the girl hadn't meant to reveal so much. To smooth over the moment, Del asked her, "What was the name of the town where you bought the stuff?"

"Northvale."

Del squinted at the map and located the small town.

"Well, if you were really in Northvale, then the next city up from there should have been the one you were looking for."

"But how could I have missed it, then?" The question was almost a wail.

Del ran her finger up the map, following the ribbon of the highway almost to the Michigan border, stopped it at another town and asked, "Are you sure it wasn't North*view?*"

The girl looked at the map, then at Del with confusion in her eyes. She said, "I don't know. Maybe it was. Oh, how could I have gotten so mixed up?"

It looked like she was about to cry again, so Del quickly responded, "It's certainly understandable. You probably didn't notice how far the man was driving because you were so upset. And the names of the towns are so similar.

"Tell you what," said Del, thoughtfully. "If you're willing to stay with me a while longer, I can teach you what you'll need to know to get along in the woods. Then when you feel like you're ready, you can continue your journey to your dad's."

Maybe that will give me time to figure out what to do with her, Del said to herself. *She's like a skittish filly. I hope she won't bolt before coming to trust me.*

The girl said nothing for the longest time, but finally nodded slightly. Del waited quietly for a moment.

"Do you know your dad's address?" she finally asked.

The girl went to the guest room and came back with a letter in her hand, the same one Del had seen on the night of the fire. The girl held it so that her fingers covered up the name and address in the center of the envelope, but showed the return address, which indeed was in the Ohio city they had been discussing. Del saw something else too. The postmark was over three years old.

This is a fine pickle! she thought. *I suppose that since it's only a couple hours away, I could drive her there. But what would we do if he doesn't live there anymore? And goodness knows whether my old car would hold up for the trip. Lord, help!*

As all this flashed through her mind in an instant, she decided to leave things as they stood for now to gain a little time to think. So she simply asked the girl to tell her about her trip through the woods and how she had come upon the garden.

At the end of the tale, Del could only shake her head and exclaim, "Child, God must really have his hand on you! Of all the places you could have ended up, here you are! And he uses the most unlikely things to accomplish his plans – even an old outhouse in the woods!"

13

Survival Skills

Later that afternoon they were once again in the woods, this time on the path that led them close to the old outhouse.

"It was built by my husband many years ago," Del explained, gesturing to it. "It was a necessity when we had three teenagers in the house and only one bathroom! He and the boys would often make the trek out here while our daughter hogged the bathroom. Was it filled with spider webs after all this time?"

The girl nodded, but stopped walking and inhaled deeply, saying, "I smell something that's nothing like an outhouse."

Del replied, "Oh, the black locust trees are blooming. They're a ways from here but their sweet scent drifts everywhere."

As they followed a path leading off in a different direction, Del began to explain various ways of capturing small animals for food, using snares, deadfalls and bolas.

"Of course," she said with a twinkle in her eye, "it helps tremendously if you start out your journey supplied with cord or rope and some type of wilderness knife or hatchet."

Then, remembering the story the girl had told about eating the rabbit, she continued with her instruction. "All wild animals are edible in an emergency, 'though you probably wouldn't want to eat skunk unless you were starving! The biggest problem is that you can't survive long on most animals. Take that rabbit you ate. It filled your stomach in an emergency, and it's a good source of protein. But a person can't live long on just rabbit. Do you know why?"

The girl shook her head, so Del said, "Fat! You need fat to stay alive, and rabbit doesn't have enough fat. Now if you could catch a beaver…"

Del resumed walking and the girl followed. *Somehow I can't imagine this child catching a beaver. I don't think she'd even have gotten a rabbit if it hadn't been virtually handed to her. But* all Del said out loud over her shoulder was, "Of course, there are other sources of fat you can find. For instance, nuts have fat *and* protein in them, but you're only gonna find them in the fall. You can also eat all birds and their eggs."

She stopped for a moment so the girl could come up beside her. "But, you know, the most abundant source of food in the wilderness is *insects.*"

She didn't look at the girl's face but kept talking while she gestured around her. "Yep, insects are all edible and they consist mostly of fat! Slugs, moths, grasshoppers, locusts…Did you know there are countries in the world where bugs are considered a delicacy? You just pull off their wings and legs and pop them right into your mouth. Oh, but you might want to avoid ants. They taste kind of bitter."

The woman stole a quick glance at the girl's face and had to bite her lip to keep from laughing. *Well, I don't want it to seem like surviving in the woods is a picnic! Everything I'm telling her is true. But even I'd have to be desperate to chow down on a cricket!*

Del started walking again and the girl followed without a comment. They soon came to an open field, where daisies bloomed in such abundance that the field looked dazzling white in the afternoon brilliance of the sun. Del headed for a patch of plain green off to the side, exclaiming, "Oh, good! It's not too late in the season for milkweed!"

She showed the girl how to select only the milkweed plants that were less than a foot tall and had stems as thick as a pencil.

"Probably the last picking of the year," she said. "Don't get the white sap on your clothes."

She put the milkweed carefully into a plastic bag and then into her backpack. Before leaving the field to head home, she pointed out the thick prickly bushes, covered with beautiful white flowers, at the very edge of the woods.

"Those are wild roses. The rose hips – their berries – are a free source of vitamin C in the winter. And they make great jelly!"

They continued walking and before long were back in the house, pulling off the milkweed leaves. The girl started to toss the leaves into the wastebasket, but Del said, "Wait! They go in the compost bucket. Could you get it? It's sitting by the door in the back room. Nothing goes to waste in my kitchen. It's all recycled back into the earth to feed the garden."

She fixed the rest of their supper before cutting the milkweed stalks into small pieces. The girl, who had been silent for quite a while, finally spoke up.

"I suppose you're going to tell me that you actually *eat* this milkweed."

Del smiled to herself, thinking, *She's probably wondering if she can trust my taste after all that talk about eating bugs.*

But all she said was, "Why, yes! Milkweed's one of my favorites. I like it even better than the vegetables I grow in the garden."

She showed the girl the proper way to prepare milkweed by pouring boiling water over it, simmering for a minute and discarding the water, and doing the same thing twice more before cooking until tender.

"Removes the milky sap which is awfully bitter," she explained while draining the milkweed and putting butter on the top to melt. "Let's eat!"

But the expression on the girl's face said, *I'm not touching that with a ten-foot pole!* She just watched the woman enjoying the milkweed, and finally asked hesitantly, "So, what does it taste like?"

Del stopped chewing, looking up with a thoughtful expression on her face.

"Well, do you like asparagus?"

"Not really."

"That's great!" Del exclaimed, emphasizing her point by spearing another milkweed stem with her fork. "Because this doesn't taste *anything* like asparagus!"

14

Del's Story

After a late breakfast the next morning, the two of them stepped out into the warm morning sun in the garden. Del had already spent time before breakfast weeding and watering, and now she looked around to see what else needed to be done. She noticed that the summer-flowering lilac tree on the right side of the backyard had opened all its frothy white blooms, and not far from it the buds on the lavender plants, held on wispy stems high above the grey-green leaves, had begun to turn, well – lavender. It was all the day-to-day changes in the garden that Del found most fascinating, and once again she thanked God for his creation that was so abundant and so diverse.

Del next checked her vegetable garden. There was not much ready to eat yet except the broccoli and lettuce. The broccoli she kept covered with a fine green netting to try to outwit the cabbage moths, but now she saw one fluttering his wings against the inside.

A lot of good this is doing if I'm just keeping them in where their favorite food is! she grumbled to herself as she lifted the net and chased the moth away.

She turned her attention to the dwarf fruit trees which were planted along the left side border. Del showed her guest the small but vigorous trees, explaining that they bore fruit of a normal size but the trees themselves stayed small enough to be manageable. Since the peaches were in need of thinning, she decided that would be today's task and set about explaining it to the girl. The teenager seemed pretty amazed at what seemed to be thousands of tiny peaches clustered on the branches of the tree.

"This tree produces so *many* peaches! Unless they're thinned, the fruits will be too small to be useful. Some will drop off by themselves, but we'll help the process along a bit," explained Del. "Did you know that each peach needs about forty leaves to supply enough food to it to develop fully?

"Don't worry," she laughed, "I'm not going to ask you to count leaves! We'll just thin the baby peaches to about six inches apart, and that should work just fine."

Del and the girl worked side by side for quite some time, dropping little fruits into a pail. Out of the blue, the girl suddenly asked, "How did you learn all that stuff about surviving in the woods?"

"Well," Del replied, her round face creasing into a smile, "my mother was Indian. 'Though I guess that's not the right term nowadays. I suppose you'd have to call us 'Native Americans.' Anyway, she was Algonquin and her people lived in Canada. And when I was young like you, I lived in a wigwam."

As she went on to relate stories about traveling down rivers in canoes, Del watched the girl out of the corner of her eye. But it wasn't until she mentioned the buffalo hunts that the girl finally caught on.

"Oh, come on!"

A hearty laugh burst from Del.

"Okay, I'll tell you the real story, 'though it's not as exciting. My mother did grow up in Canada. But when she married my father they moved to a farm here in Michigan. I've been told that I look a lot like my mother, but I seem to have my father's outgoing personality. He was Irish – an unlikely combination, don't you think?"

Del paused in her work for a moment, remembering.

"My mother loved our farm, but she would get restless sometimes to be out in the wild. So she would take me with her on long trips into the woods. She taught me so many things. Sometimes we'd stay out for several days. My father was always anxious for us to return, but he never tried to stop my mother from doing what she wanted to do."

Del's eyes had a far-away look in them as she smiled, saying, "They loved each other very much."

The girl picked up the pail they were using and scooped up a handful of tiny peaches, letting them flow through her fingers again and again. Del watched her, understanding her fascination with the tiny silvery fruits that had the silkiness of kitten's fur.

Suddenly the girl, her face still bent over the pail, said quietly, "My name isn't really Ariel. It's Mara."

Maybe she's starting to trust me, thought Del, but all she said was, "Well, where'd you get the name Ariel from?"

The girl brushed her hair back from her hot, flushed face and replied, "It was just from a movie I loved when I was a kid."

When she was a kid! How old could she be now? So Del asked and was surprised to find out that Mara was sixteen, "...and a half!" she was pointedly told. Then Del said something the girl wasn't expecting.

"I never did think your name was Ariel."

It was the girl's turn to look surprised, and Del explained, "Your backpack has the initials 'M.R.' on it."

She went on, "But that's okay. My name's not really Del, either!"

Mara looked confused, so Del said, "My given name's Christine. Now I ask you – do I look like a Christine?" She chuckled when the girl smiled and shook her head.

"My mother loved flowers too," Del said. "When I was little I used to play in her gardens all the time. I'd play with the seeds and pin little flowers in my hair. My favorite ones of all were the delphiniums, so my father teased me by calling me 'my little Delphinium.' Soon my little brother was calling me 'Delphie' and eventually no one called me Christine any more!"

Now Del's broad smile faded and she sighed as she continued her story.

"My mother died from cancer when I was just a little older than you are. I helped take care of my brother for about six years, and then my father..." She hesitated a moment before saying, "...died."

Neither talked any more while finishing up the last of the crowded peaches. Del took the pail and emptied it onto the compost pile, then started into the house for lunch. Mara, following her, broke the silence with the question, "How did your father die?"

Del stopped walking, turning slightly around towards the girl, before replying softly and with pain in her voice, "I killed him."

15

The Story Continues

Upon seeing the look of shock on the girl's face, Del quickly added, "Not on purpose, of course." She suggested that they get lunch ready and she'd tell the rest of the story.

"It was so difficult helping take care of my mother during the final months of her illness. When she died, I was just devastated. But going to school and taking care of my younger brother kept me pretty busy. I think my father suffered the most. He was never quite the same after she died. He didn't have the heart any more to keep up with the farm, so after a while we sold it and moved to a small nearby city. He wasn't old by any means, but his health deteriorated to the point where I drove him everywhere.

"I was driving him to the doctor one day when I got careless, and made a left turn in front of an oncoming car."

Del stopped talking and it was obvious that, even though the accident had happened a long time ago, it was still difficult to talk about. But after sighing deeply she continued, "My father was killed instantly. And I was in the hospital for several weeks."

She set the food on the table, and then they were seated and began to eat. Or rather Mara did. Del just stared out the big window to the garden where a light breeze rippled through the flowers. Behind her little round glasses, her eyes had become shiny with tears. It was a few minutes before she spoke again.

"My aunt came to see me in the hospital. She was my father's sister – a wonderful, loving woman. She kept telling me that it was just an accident, that these things happen sometimes, that it wasn't my fault. But, of course, I kept blaming myself. I felt so guilty. My aunt wanted me and my brother to come and live with her, and that's what we did for a time after I got out of the hospital. But my feelings were so overwhelming that it wasn't long before I ran away."

Del stopped, and after a moment picked up her fork to begin eating. Even the tragic story wasn't enough to keep her from her lunch, because Del did enjoy her food. As she ate, she reflected to herself, *Maybe sharing my own story will help this child to realize that everyone has problems, and running away isn't the answer.*

But Mara only asked, "Where did you go?"

"To New York City. You know, in a way you were much smarter than I was. If I had run into the woods maybe I wouldn't have gotten into so much trouble. In the city it was pretty awful, and after awhile I really hit bottom."

And, no, I won't tell her the worst thing.

Del, for some reason, felt uneasy at the last thought. But the opportunity passed when the girl, having finished her lunch, said, "Your brother. Whatever happened to him?"

Del shook her head sadly.

"My brother lived with my aunt for years, but I guess all the tragedy in his life affected his mind. He became a drifter, never able to hold onto a job or settle down in one place for long. Years later, after I had married and gotten my life in order, I reconnected with my aunt and tried to track down my brother. He occasionally would touch base with her so I'd send her money for him.

"One time I was actually able to find him, but our reunion went bad. He was angry at me. I guess he blames me for our father's death. I'm a little afraid of him, so I always hope he doesn't find out where I live. My aunt passed away years ago so there's no longer any connection there. Maybe some of my cousins keep in touch with him."

Del shrugged. Since there were no other questions from the girl, she put the dishes in the sink and went to pray her Rosary.

Mara sat on the floor, trying to entice the kittens out of their box under the table. Ginger was a little bolder than the others, hanging her head and paws over the edge of the hole until she fell out, *plop,* right onto the wooden floor. Mara picked her up and soothed her, then lifted out the other kittens and put all three in her lap. They were tiny yet, their eyes just recently open, and their fuzzy fur was so soft and fine that it was barely felt against one's hand. As she set each onto its feet on the floor, she marveled that the kittens seemed as if they hardly weighed anything at all.

She smiled to see their stumbling footsteps, and how they bumped into each other or fell forward onto their pink noses. Their bellies, filled with Mama Cat's nourishing milk, were round as balls, and their spiky little tails stood straight up. The girl noticed that the third kitten had some brown undertones in its dark fur. Combined with the white patches it made her think of chocolate milk, so she decided to call this one "Coco."

After a long while, Del jumped up from her easy chair, saying, "Time to go wilding!" Mara carefully placed the kittens back in their box and followed the woman out to the woods. They didn't stay out long today, for the sun had gotten very hot and Del had some things to do around the house. When they had returned inside, Del began her chores and asked Mara, "Say, why don't you run out and get the mail for me?"

16

The Mailbox

Mara stepped out the front door onto a small cement porch, musing that it seemed forever since she'd been anywhere but this woman's house and back garden. *And the woods, of course.* Deep in thought, she jumped off the top step onto the ground, and started to follow the sidewalk out to the road when suddenly she stopped dead in her tracks.

What was it, she thought, *that felt so weird, sort of out of place?*

She turned around and looked at the house, then surveyed the front yard. Suddenly it hit her. *Why, it's just so* ordinary *out here! Just like millions of other front yards!*

Oh, not that it wasn't nice. The house, one-story high and long across the front, had light-colored brick halfway up with white aluminum siding above it. The window shutters and the front door were painted slate blue, and evergreen bushes ran along the foundation of the house with a few flowers blooming in front of them. On the left side of the house were some tire tracks in the grass, leading to a high wooden fence with a closed gate. To her right was the garage, with large flowering shrubs on the other side of the cement driveway.

Nice, but so ordinary, she thought again.

She could see the top of the windmill, towering high over the garage roof. Except for that, this house could be like any other. *Standing here, you'd never guess that there's a remarkable garden in the backyard.* The girl reflected that she had been so immersed in beautiful flowers she had almost forgotten there was a "normal" world out there.

My mother used to like flowers, she remembered. *At one time I even had a little garden of my own.* Perhaps that was why she was genuinely enjoying the work in the garden, learning the names of the flowers and all. *I guess it's been sort of a healing place for me to be.*

But, Mara said to herself, still standing in the front yard looking at the house, *I'm not so sure about this lady! She sure is odd. I mean, really, who would ever think about eating weeds, not to mention some of the other things she talked about!* At that thought, her stomach felt a bit queasy.

Well, okay, I'll admit that 'most everything she's cooked hasn't been too bad. But she does such strange things! She has these little paper cups she keeps in every room of the house that she calls "bug cups." Instead of killing any spiders that get into the house, she actually captures them in the cups and throws them out the door! She says, "Spiders are our friends." Well, they're not my *friends!*

Mara shuffled her feet on the sidewalk as her thoughts tumbled on.

Yesterday she was singing at the top of her lungs, "Home, home and deranged, where the deer have the antelope's brains!" When I asked her, "What are *you* singing?" *she just laughed and said her husband used to make up funny lyrics to songs.*

And then there was today, when I asked her if she had a TV. "Whatever would I do with a TV?" she says. And when I said, "Well, don't you at least want to know what's going on in the world?" she says, "What for?" Says she listens to the radio when she wakes up in the morning, "just to make sure the world's still there," as she puts it. Really, how can you live without a TV?

The girl frowned.

And, good grief, is there anyone in the world who prays as much as she does? Prayer after lunch, prayer after supper, and I'll just bet she prays in the morning before I'm up! It's God this, and God that. She's driving me crazy!

But at that last thought the girl felt slightly ashamed of herself. Del *had* been awfully kind to her. It was just necessary to keep your wits about you in this place, because one never knew what would pop up next.

She swung around and marched down the sidewalk, then stopped abruptly. Oh my gosh, what was *this?*

A big mailbox stood near the edge of the road. "Big" didn't adequately describe it, though. Mara thought it just might be possible for her to crawl inside and take a nap.

She looked at the side of the giant mailbox and saw that it had been painted – a long time ago, evidenced by its fading colors – with red flowers on a green vine that curled around the bottom edge and clambered over the mailbox door. Under the picture of the flowers were painted the words, "Windmill Gardens."

Why should I be surprised at this thing when nothing else around here is normal?

She sighed to herself, then, before opening the mailbox, took a few minutes to look around out of curiosity. The dirt road, which dead-ended just past Del's property on one side, ran off in the other direction in a straight line. Looking down it, she could just make out in the distance a tall white house with a grey barn behind it.

That must be where those people, Richard and Ann, live.

There wasn't much else to be seen except woods lining the road on both sides. Tall trees on both sides of Del's property gave a person a feeling of being in sort of a valley, just a house and an oasis of flowers in the midst of ordinary greenery.

Finally, Mara opened the gigantic mailbox and pulled out a brown corrugated box and a handful of mail. She took the items into the house and handed them to Del.

"Oh, good!" the woman exclaimed. "My package finally arrived."

Wielding a pair of sharp scissors she soon revealed the box's contents – more garden supplies!

"Why," asked Mara, "do you have such a huge mailbox?"

Del replied that she ordered a lot of items by mail order. There wasn't a big selection in the nearby town so she liked the variety and convenience offered by ordering through catalogs.

"I buy most of my garden stuff this way, and it's a great way to get lots of good books!"

"So where in the world did you find such a big mailbox?" the girl inquired.

Del answered, "Through a mail-order catalog, of course!"

With that she disappeared through the kitchen doorway to start the evening meal.

17

Sunday

I can't believe, the girl was thinking, *that I'm actually bouncing along the road in this old boat.* It wasn't exactly a boat, for it certainly had four wheels and looked enough like a car. But "boat" was how she first thought of the big old automobile the first time she saw it sitting in Del's garage.

She reflected to herself that the morning had begun normally enough, with Del fixing a late breakfast for the two of them after Mara had climbed out of bed. All of a sudden, Del had announced in a loud voice, "Well, today's Sunday!"

I guess I've sort of lost track of the days, the girl thought. *It's so-o-o exciting around here!*

"I go to church on Sundays," Del continued, "and you're welcome to come along with me if you'd like." Her brow furrowed, she thought for a moment before adding, "I'm Catholic, but there are a few other churches in our small town. Let's see, there's a Lutheran one and a Presbyterian one, and I believe there might be a non-denominational one that's not too far away. I could drop you off at one of those for a service if you'd like."

But Mara just shrugged.

"It doesn't matter. I can go with you." *Anything would be more interesting than sitting around here by myself.* Then another thought occurred to her.

"Won't people want to know who I am or why I'm here?" she asked nervously.

But Del shook her head.

"I doubt if anyone will pay much attention. Most of the people are friendly enough, but they keep to themselves. Besides, I often have relatives come and visit. Remember me telling you about my aunt? Some of her grandkids have stayed with me in past summers, helping in the garden and learning about the wild, just like you. So I don't think it will be a problem."

"So which service are we going to?"

"Well," Del replied, "there's one at twelve o'clock and one at noon. Which would you prefer?"

Puzzled, Mara just said, "Huh?" which caused Del to break out in a hearty laugh. The girl got up and took her dishes to the sink, rolling her eyes. *She thinks even the littlest things are funny!*

Del explained, "Years ago, we used to have a priest just for our church. Back then we had a lot more activity going on. But the priest we have now takes care of our church and the one in the next town, so there's only one Mass here on Sundays. The other church has an early one and we have the later one. Let's go water the flowers. Then we'll get dressed for church."

After they had come back into the house from the backyard, Del found a pair of tan pants in her son's room that looked better than the jeans that Mara had been wearing. Del herself exchanged her oversized work shirts and grass-stained pants for a flower-print top and a pair of black dress pants.

She still looks like Del, thought Mara. *But the black moccasins are definitely an improvement over those rubber garden shoes she always wears.*

Del took a ring of keys off a hook in the back room and opened a door Mara hadn't noticed before. They stepped down into the attached garage. The woman switched on an overhead light bulb, but it didn't actually cast much light into the darkness of the space. To their left was another door with a window, and through it the girl could see the brightness of the late morning sun shimmering on the kaleidoscope of flowers in the backyard.

Inside the garage, Mara squinted her eyes in the dim light and could make out a long workbench and crowded wooden shelves. Del was saying, "You can see now why my husband felt a need to build a workshop just for himself. He said I took over everything in here."

She pointed to cardboard boxes filled with sand, to pails of silica gel and other equipment cluttering the garage.

"All this stuff is for drying flowers. This clothesline," she gestured over their heads, "is where I hang flowers to air-dry. I have a fan which circulates the air so they don't get moldy while drying. Some flowers need to be immersed in the silica or sand while drying in order to maintain their colors. And here is a drying screen," she said, pointing to something that looked to Mara like a mesh sweater-dryer, "where you poke stems of flowers through so their heads stay on top to dry."

This looks complicated, Mara was thinking, just as Del exclaimed, "Oh, gracious, it's getting late! Let's get going!" She pushed a button on the wall and the garage door began to rise.

Mara blinked in the sudden bright light entering the dim interior of the garage, and then she blinked again when she saw the car. It did resemble a boat. It was huge and long and low. *Just how old is this thing?*

The car was an indescribable shade of green. The back section of the top at one time had been covered with foam rubber, but now the pearl-green plastic coating had torn or rotted in places and the foam was poking out. Some of the metal roof showed through, rusty in the spots where even the foam had fallen off.

"Climb in," called Del in a merry voice, so Mara climbed into the passenger's side and ran her hand over the soft velvet seats. *They're green, too! And so is the dashboard, the steering wheel, the carpet...*

Del backed the car out of the garage onto the driveway and pointed the control at the garage door, watching with evident fascination while the door slowly made its way down.

"My husband installed that for me," she said, turning to the girl. "When he found out he had cancer he tried to make it as easy as possible for me to go on living here. Believe me, my back is grateful for that garage door opener!"

Now they were speeding down the bumpy dirt road on the way to town. *Doesn't this thing have springs?* Mara wondered. *If she would just slow down a little! But I think she's trying to stay ahead of the dust cloud we're raising. Wouldn't you know? The air conditioner's broken and the windows are wide open.*

As they got closer to town and there were more houses, Mara slunk down in her seat, a little embarrassed to be seen in the "boat." She didn't slink too far, though, as she was curious to see what the town was like. But one could say there wasn't much to be seen. They passed only a few stores and a gas station before Del turned sharply into a parking lot beside a small, rectangular building with a low ridged roof.

This is a church? Mara wondered. But as they hurried around to the front door, she saw a small sign boldly proclaiming, "St. Bernard Catholic Church." She suppressed a smile as an image of large dogs marching into church went through her mind.

Mara paused for a moment just inside the door to let her eyes adjust from the brightness outside. However, Del hurried up the short aisle and into a pew, so the girl followed. They didn't seem to be late, as people were just sitting there waiting. Del knelt down, not paying attention to anything but her prayers, while Mara sat and looked around with interest. The small church was only half full, and everyone was dressed rather casually in the summer heat. She glanced across the aisle and noticed a tall, good-looking man with dark hair staring right at her. Catching her eye, he grinned and winked and she hurriedly looked elsewhere. *That must be that Richard guy,* she thought, perusing with sudden great interest the hanging ceiling lights and the rest of the interior.

Brightly-colored stained glass windows lined both of the side walls. These windows were not the pictures of saints that one usually associates with Catholic churches, but rather were made up of small yellow and orange squares set in vertical flowing patterns like dancing flames. The light through the colorful windows shone warmly on the dark-stained wood of the pews. Up front by the altar, Mara could see large vases of flowers set in a semi-circle on the floor. Not far from the altar was something like a wooden lectern, and on the back wall opposite it hung a golden-doored box with a candle, glowing inside a red glass holder, mounted nearby. She noticed that behind the altar seemed to be a mosaic of some sort, set with small shiny pieces of tile.

Her eye was caught by someone inching toward the small organ console set off to the left side near the front. *That lady has to be a hundred years old,* she surmised, watching the small, hunched-over figure with white hair carefully settle herself at the organ and turn on the switch. *Oh, wonderful. I'll just bet she plays as s-l-o-w as she walks.*

Now, that turned out to be quite a surprise. After limbering up her fingers by wiggling them above the keyboard, the organist launched into the first hymn at an alarmingly rapid tempo. Mara stood up when everyone else did and tried to follow along in the hymnal Del handed her, but she couldn't make head nor tail of the unfamiliar melody which was speeding by so rapidly. After four verses at such a pace, everyone seemed a bit out of breath and happy to replace the hymnals in their holders. Del glanced at Mara with eyes that were brimming with suppressed laughter, but the girl turned her attention to the priest who had come to the altar.

He was a rather short man with red hair wearing some kind of green robe. He began to lead prayers and Mara suddenly lost interest. The entire service lasted less than an hour, but none of it made much sense to the girl. Sure, a guy got up and read from the Bible. *That* she recognized. But the priest's talk, short as it was, was not very interesting, and the rest of the prayers and all the other stuff they did – stand, sit, kneel, make funny arm movements – *who could figure it all out?*

Mara occasionally looked over at Del, but the woman seemed engrossed in what was going on up front. The girl stole another glance at Richard and noticed next to him a boy who was maybe ten or eleven. The organist continued to massacre the music. Mara recognized the hymn "Amazing Grace," but she couldn't get the words out fast enough to join in. When everyone started filing out of the pews to form a line going up to the front, she also stood up. But Del put a hand on her arm and whispered, "Wait here for me. I'll be back from Communion in a minute."

Mara, settling back down on the uncomfortable wooden pew, noticed that Del had left a prayer book on the seat. She picked it up to leaf through it and a small card fell out. On one side of the card was a picture of an old white-haired man with the strange name "Padre Pio" written underneath. On the opposite side were the following words:

"Stay with me, Lord, for it is necessary to have you present so that I do not forget you.

"Stay with me, Lord, for you are my light and without you, I am in darkness.

"Stay with me, Lord, so that I hear your voice and follow you…"

Stay with me? Is that supposed to be a prayer? How weird! Maybe this church is some sort of a cult or something. But by then Del had returned and the service was finishing. They raced through another song and it was over. People began to leave.

"Come on," whispered Del, "I want you to meet Father Mike."

She led the way to the door where the priest was greeting people. When he saw Del approaching, he got a wary look in his eyes and took a small step backwards. It didn't help. Good old warm-hearted Del still managed to smother him in a bear hug, and only let him go when he managed to gasp out, "So! Del! Are you going to lock up today?"

She laughed and declared, "Of course, Father! I always do, don't I? I want you to meet Mara." She turned around, looking for the girl who was hanging back, and drew her forward with her hand. "Mara is helping me in the garden."

Father Mike made some small talk, but seemed happy when Del let him escape in a few minutes. Next, Richard and his son came up to her and she introduced them to Mara. With a broad smile, the woman demanded to know just when Richard was going to deliver that straw he had promised her.

"I'll get it to you," promised her neighbor, "now that I'm done rescuing damsels in distress!" He winked again at the girl and she ducked her head in embarrassment.

"Come on," said Del to Mara, leading her back inside the church. "Help me get things cleaned up and then we'll go home."

While they straightened hymnals and picked up, Del asked Mara what she thought of their organist. *I don't want to be unkind,* thought the girl, *but...*She didn't have to utter a word because the look on her face said it all. Del burst out laughing.

"Father has asked her to slow it down time and time again. But she says if she goes slower, her arthritis makes her fingers hurt too much and she makes more mistakes."

They finished their work by checking the flower bouquets. Then Del asked Mara if she would mind waiting for just a few minutes so she could pray in front of the tabernacle. So the girl took a seat in one of the pews while Del dragged a chair over in front of the golden-doored box on the wall and sat down heavily.

Mara closed her eyes in the silence of the sunlit church, thinking things over and wondering if she should make an attempt to pray too. But her thoughts wandered back to her childhood when she used to go to church services with her mother and father.

Those were certainly happier times, she thought. *How could things turn out so wrong? Is there something I could've done differently?* As she struggled within herself to set aside the hurtful memories of the past, the worries of the present took over.

What am I going to do next? How long will I be able to stay here before moving on? What if my dad has moved away? And then, unbidden, *what if he doesn't want me?*

With that, pain seared her heart and tears trickled down her face. She couldn't have known that Del, at that very moment, was interceding for her before the throne of Mercy, begging her Jesus for grace and guidance for this little lost soul.

18

The Girl Tells Her Story

Later that Sunday afternoon, they were seated at the kitchen table with large steel bowls in their laps. A casserole was baking in the oven for supper, and the aroma of onions, fresh garlic and tomato sauce hung in the air. The two of them had just spent more than an hour in Del's strawberry garden, searching for the glistening red fruits.

Now an overflowing quart of washed berries sat next to them on the table. Mara was slicing each one into a bowl on her lap, while Del cut shortening into flour in a bowl on her own lap. When she had suggested after returning from church that they could make some strawberry shortcake for supper, the girl had actually smiled. Del was happy to see that, because Mara had seemed so quiet and distant in the car on the way home. The kittens were out of their box and playing on the kitchen floor, entertaining both of them with their antics.

Del's hands were working on the shortcake but her thoughts were on the One who was always with her, even when he seemed not to be.

Lord, you're not giving me any answers here. I'd just like to know what to do, and instead I'm bumbling my way along. I'm perfectly capable of messing things up on my own, so I really need your help. For a few moments Del kept pouring out her heart to God. *Okay, okay, I do trust you. I don't hear your voice but I know, my Jesus, that you guide me. I guess it's my job to keep praying.*

Minute by minute, the silence in the kitchen seemed to be growing, so at last Del cautiously threw out a question.

"Do you go to church much?"

At first it didn't seem as if an answer was forthcoming, but finally Mara replied, "I used to." She glanced up at Del quickly, then back to the job at hand.

57

"We used to go when I was little. I got baptized when I was about ten. I remember getting dunked under the water. But it wasn't long after that my parents stopped going to church."

She paused and took a deep breath. Suddenly it seemed as if she wanted to share her story with the woman, who listened patiently as the girl unburdened her heart.

"We used to be so happy, my mom and dad and me! My dad took us on camping trips all the time. He was the one who showed me the best way to build a fire for cooking, and how to make sure it was completely out so you wouldn't burn down the woods. And we'd lie in our tent at night and tell stories and listen to the crickets. It was so much fun."

Mara set the bowl of sliced strawberries on the table. She had tears in her eyes. Del didn't know whether or not she'd continue but, after a long pause, she did.

"I don't really know what happened, but my parents started to argue all the time. And when I was twelve, my dad left one day and didn't come home. He called and wrote me letters for awhile, but then he just stopped."

Del thought of the envelope the girl had shown her. Was it possible that this letter, over three years old, was the last time her father had contacted her? *Why, Lord,* she thought, *are the kids always the ones who bear the brunt of the parents' problems?*

The girl, perhaps to hide her tears, had slid down onto the floor to play with the kittens, so Del didn't pursue the subject any further. The casserole was nearly done, and Del wanted to bake the shortcake and whip up some of Richard's fantastically rich cream for the dessert topping.

It wasn't until they had finished supper and had licked clean the bowl of whipped cream, that Del decided to bring up a topic that had been bothering her a lot. *She's been gone from home more than a week now. Someone must be frantic about her disappearance.* As they washed and dried the dirty dishes, Del gingerly broached the topic.

"Don't you think your mother must be awfully worried about you?"

The swift answer came vehemently, startling Del.

"My mother doesn't care!"

Surprised, Del stopped what she was doing and stared, uncomprehending, at the girl.

Her mother doesn't care? How could that be?

The girl tossed her head angrily and, with her eyes narrowed a little, repeated, "My mother doesn't care." But this time the emphatic words seemed directed more at the woman in front of her.

"What do you mean, child?" Del asked.

"Just what I said! My mother doesn't care about me! She doesn't listen to me, she doesn't believe me when I try to tell her things..." Mara's voice trailed off as she fought to keep control of its trembling.

"Well," said Del soothingly, "most moms really do care. But often they're caught up in their own troubles and it's hard for them to notice when their kids are hurting."

The girl just glared at Del with brimming eyes and threw her dish towel on the counter next to the sink, saying, "I'm tired. I'm going to go to bed early tonight." She quickly left the kitchen and Del heard the bedroom door close.

That evening, Del rubbed her eyes in weariness as she sat at her kitchen table with her prayer book open in front of her. *Hide her in the shadow of your wings, Lord,* she prayed from Psalm 17. *Protect her from any further pain in her life. Help her to find strength in you. I don't know, Lord, if that was the right thing for me to ask her. You are going to have to put your words in my mouth, since I seem to have blown it!*

But Del was a woman wise with constant prayer and dependence on God. Regardless of what she had just prayed, she instinctively knew that sometimes a person, tied up inside with so much hurt, first needs to get angry to be able to let the words tumble out.

Why do young people think they have to carry their burdens all by themselves? Perhaps she'll feel better now that she's opened up a bit. I just ask to be able to help her in some way. Oh, my Jesus, you have been so merciful to me. Help me to extend that mercy to another in your name.

19

Leave It To Cleavers

"Time to get back to work!" Del announced the next morning after breakfast. "Yesterday was my day off. The only garden chores I do on Sunday are watering whatever needs it, and picking what's ripe. After all, God had a day of rest after creating his beautiful garden and everything in it." She stopped to grin at Mara. "So I figure I can do the same!"

Del had already decided during that morning's prayer time that she would wait for the girl, if she was so inclined, to reopen yesterday's conversation. Mara had dark circles under her eyes, but otherwise seemed all right, although even more quiet than usual.

Del declared, "I want to show you something."

She went into her back room and unpinned some papers that were hanging from a corkboard on the door leading to the garage.

"These are what I call my 'maps'," she explained, spreading them out on the table and settling herself into one of the wooden chairs.

"This largest paper you see here is an overview of the whole backyard. Each smaller garden is drawn on it, and the letter on each – A, B, C and so forth – corresponds to one of these other papers, where you'll find the name and location of every plant in that garden. On the back of each," she said, turning one over to show the girl, "is a complete list of all the particulars about those plants – their watering needs, bloom times, stuff like that."

The girl seemed amazed at how many papers there were. There had to be dozens of individual gardens shown here!

"I used to know all this stuff by heart, but each year I find I need to write down more and more of it," Del said with a smile. "But I plan to keep gardening 'til I'm literally pushing up daisies!"

Mara asked, "How do you do all this by yourself?"

"Oh, most of the time I'm fine. The hardest work is in the fall when there's cleanup to be done, and in the spring when I do the planting. I usually hire a young man from town to help me with those things and also with the pruning in late winter. Most of my plants are perennials which come back every year, but I always put in some annuals, too. And then there are the vegetables to be planted every spring.

"It *is* nice, though," she stated, touching Mara's arm lightly, "to have someone helping me who likes flowers. Feel free to take these maps out into the garden any time you want, to learn which flower is which. Now let's go out and spread the straw which Richard dropped off this morning."

They stepped out the door into an exquisitely beautiful morning. The sky was blue as only a June sky can be. Little puffs of clouds scudded along in the light breeze that had already dried the dew on the plants. Fat fuzzy bumblebees were flocking to the red fragrant flowers of the bee balm. The bright poppies were waving their eye-catching orange and black blooms, as if to say, "Look at me!" while the wind rippled the deep purple of the salvia until it resembled ocean waves.

Del and the girl worked for some time, taking handfuls of yellow straw from the opened bales and tucking them around and under plants, mulching to conserve water and help prevent weeds. One might think that a flower garden with straw spread over it would not look very attractive at all. But the plants in Del's garden had grown so thickly together over the years that, if truth be told, not a whole lot of the mulch was visible.

The paths did not have straw on them but were mostly wood-chipped, and a few of the narrowest ones had a low-growing ground cover with tiny leaves and even tinier white flowers. Mara had noticed that the same plant grew between the patio stones and she asked Del what it was.

"Oh, that's creeping thyme," Del answered, on her knees examining the bright flowers of the gaillardia. "It sure smells nice when you walk on it, doesn't it?

"You know what?" she suddenly exclaimed. "I think we'd better weed the raspberries next and then mulch them. Last time I looked the cleavers were taking over."

She led the way to where the berry canes grew along the fence behind the fruit trees and pointed out the long, spindly, light-green weeds clinging to them.

61

"Have to get these out now before they go to seed or I'll have a real mess next year. Here, better put this on." She tossed one of her vinyl-coated garden gloves to Mara and put the other one on her own left hand.

"Why are these weeds called 'cleavers'?" Mara asked as she pulled the first one with a gloved hand.

"Because," said Del, "they *cleave* to everything!"

She threw a weed at the girl where it stuck fast to her T-shirt. So Mara tossed one at Del and it stuck in her hair. Del threw another one and so did Mara, and before long they both had green strands covering their shirts and hanging down over their faces, making them look a little like swamp creatures who had just emerged from the deep.

They were laughing and trying to pull the tenacious weeds off themselves, when Del caught her breath and said seriously, "You know, these things are edible. Shall we cook some up for supper?"

At that, the girl just lost it. She dropped down on the ground, laughing so hard she was bent over double, holding her stomach. There was nothing for Del to do but join in.

After quite some time, spent and wiping tears from their eyes, they plucked the last weedy pieces from their hair and clothing. Gathering the pesky plants in a basket, they took them over to the other side of the garden by the windmill and tossed them on the compost pile.

That was fun, thought Del with a broad smile. *It was good to hear her laugh.*

That made what happened next even more surprising.

In a half-circle around the compost pile were tall wire cages, each supporting a short but robust tomato plant. Del always planted her tomatoes in such a manner so they could draw nutrients from the pile as the waste material began to break down. Now she stopped to admire her plants, especially the first one which was, by far, the largest.

"Hello, Tom, how are you doing today?" she addressed her prized tomato in a booming voice.

The girl, who had been bent over a short distance away examining a cucumber vine, straightened up suddenly and shouted, "Wha…?!"

She glanced quickly around the garden while Del, her mouth hanging open a bit, just stared at the girl in amazement.

Mara looked as white as a sheet and her eyes were darting here and there with a look of sheer terror in them.

After a minute, seeing nothing but the peaceful garden with birds circling overhead, she directed her gaze back to Del and demanded, "*Who* were you talking to?"

Keeping her eyes on the unpredictable girl, Del gestured to the wire cage next to her and replied, "Just my tomato plant."

The girl took several deep breaths to calm herself, then took a step closer to Del and in a tightly-controlled voice asked, "Why in the world would you name a plant *Tom?*"

Del kept staring at her while trying to figure out what was going on. After a short pause, she said lightly, "Well, I thought that Tom was a good name for a *tom*ato plant. But, if you'd prefer, I'll call it 'Big Red' from now on." And Del kept talking, trying to bring some ease to the girl and give her time to collect herself.

"There are a lot of people around this town who try to be the first to get a ripe tomato from their garden. It's turned into sort of a contest every year. That's why this tomato plant you see here on the end is so much bigger, because it's the one I've been babying along. I cover this spot with black plastic in the spring so the ground will warm up quickly. Then I set out, as early as I possibly can, my biggest tomato plant that I've grown from seed. Around it, I set plastic jugs with water in 'em. The water is warmed by the sun every day and releases the heat at night so the plant doesn't get chilled."

Del pointed to the baby fruits on the plant, saying, "See, it's worked pretty well, as all the others are just starting to flower now." But she realized that the girl didn't seem to be listening any longer. Mara was standing with her head bent, rubbing her hand across her eyes.

Del waited patiently, hoping that she'd explain why she had had such a strange reaction to such innocuous words. But it soon became obvious that nothing else was forthcoming, so the woman, figuring that good food could fix nearly every problem, took the girl into the house to have lunch.

20

A Cherry Interesting Conversation

"I don't believe in God."

This softly-spoken but unexpected statement was tossed out by the girl as they sat the next afternoon at the kitchen table, sorting through several large bowls of bright red cherries. The two of them had spent half the morning gathering the marble-sized fruits from a row of cherry bushes along the side fence. Del intended to remove the pits from some of the cherries and make a cobbler with them. The fruits were so small that it was too labor-intensive to pit them all, so the rest she would cook up and strain for jelly.

As their hands had been busy sorting the cherries and selecting only the biggest and best for the cobbler, Del had been speaking about God's love for us as evidenced in all the beautiful flowers and variety of fruits. So when the girl threw out, "I don't believe in God," Del's thoughts were startled, even though her hands barely paused in their work.

Not believe in God? Why, Del couldn't even imagine such a thing! She knew that God was nearer to her than her own beating heart. Sure, there was a time in her own life, when, hardly older than this child here, she had turned her back on God and walked away from him. *And, boy, what a mess I made, trying to do it all my way!*

But even while rebelling against him, she always believed that he was real. Not to believe in God! *Good grief, that would make "me" the center of my own universe!* Del, in essence a very humble person, was horrified at the thought.

All this passed through her mind in a split second, and it was followed by the conviction that it did no good to argue with a person about his or her beliefs. So, continuing to sort cherries, Del just asked in an offhand way, "Why don't you believe in God?"

Perhaps the girl was a little nonplussed that Del, who talked about God at the drop of a hat, didn't disagree with her, but asked her a question as if she really cared what the girl thought. It took Mara a moment before she finally answered the question with another question.

"If there really is a God and he loves us like you say, then why do so many awful things happen to people?"

"What kinds of things, child?"

"Well," the girl said slowly, looking down at the bowl on her lap, "people who haven't done anything wrong get hurt by other people in their life. Why doesn't God stop it?"

Del suspected that this question went deeper than it sounded. She prayed quickly for guidance while saying, "Well, I guess because God gave us the great gift of free will. A person is free to choose to do good in life, or do wrong. If God took away the consequences, like an innocent person getting hurt, what would happen to the first person's free will?"

She waited for Mara to sort this out in her mind, and in a minute the girl asked, "So, because of our free will, God is helpless to do anything?"

"Well, no, he's hardly helpless. He often sends just the right person into a situation to help someone who's been hurt. You know, God doesn't cause bad things to happen, but he can always bring some good out of bad situations."

Del was pointedly trying to shed some light on whatever trouble Mara was facing. But she wasn't sure the girl was really picking up on any of it, because Mara tossed her hair back from her face before looking at Del somewhat defiantly and asking, "Well, then, what about all the earthquakes and hurricanes and other natural disasters that can wipe out whole villages of people, especially in poor countries? You can't tell me *that* has anything to do with free will!"

Del didn't answer while she went to get another bowl in which to put the pitted cherries. She showed the girl how to pop out the cherry pits, then threw out a question of her own.

"Tell me, Mara, if you were God, what kind of a world would you create?"

So the girl painted a lovely word picture of a wonderful place to live, a place where people really loved each other, where no one ever got hurt and each person had everything they needed.

"And it would be filled with beautiful flowers, just like your backyard!"

At that, Del laughed heartily and exclaimed, "Why, child, God *did* create such a world! It's called heaven! This earth is only our temporary home. God wants us to live in heaven – our eternal home – with him, where it will be even better than what you described."

But Mara wasn't convinced.

"Why should I believe that this place you call heaven exists?"

Del stopped working on the cherries for a minute while she thought. Then she asked something totally unexpected.

"What do you think of my front yard?"

Mara, caught a bit off balance, hesitated before saying, "Well, I guess it's okay. Quite honestly, it's rather ordinary-looking, compared to the backyard." She looked at Del suspiciously and asked, "What does that have to do with anything?"

Del had a twinkle in her eye as she replied, "What if you had come to my house from the road instead of the woods, and all you had seen was the front yard? Wouldn't you have thought that it seemed a pleasant enough place? All the while, unbeknownst to you, hidden behind the fence was the most fantastic garden you could ever have imagined.

"Well, this earth," Del indicated the whole world with a sweep of her cherry-stained hand, "like my front yard, seems like a nice enough place to be most of the time. But there's a more wonderful place called 'heaven' that's hidden from our view for now."

Mara had finished her bowl of cherries and set it on the table. She leaned forward on her folded arms and gazed out the window. Birds were circling above the inviting garden, occasionally landing and flying off with some prize in their beaks. There was a sense of tranquility in the rays of sunshine that reflected off the light-colored wood chips. Pathways were turned into molten rivers of light, flowing between patches of cheerful flowers.

The girl looked as if she would like to absorb the garden into herself, in order to find the peace that she so desperately needed. In a quiet voice, almost to herself, she said, "I don't know if I deserve such a place."

Del was silent for a few moments, reflecting on the twists and turns this conversation had taken. There had been something in the girl's first statement, about not believing in God, that made Del think there was a great deal of hurt underneath. Perhaps the girl really meant, "I don't believe that God loves me." So the woman who knew the healing power of God's love and mercy in her own life attempted to answer the unspoken pain behind the words.

"There's not one of us that deserves it, child. But we can't even imagine how much God loves us and wants us with him in heaven. That's why Jesus came into this world. He died on the cross to save us from our sins and prove that God loves us."

Unsure of how much the girl had picked up in her childhood Sunday school lessons, she asked the girl, "What were you taught about believing in Jesus?"

Mara thought a minute, then shrugged her shoulders, replying, "That whoever believed in him would have eternal life."

"True enough," Del said, "but what does 'believing' really mean?"

The girl seemed unsure, so the woman went on, "Believing, or having faith, isn't just a thought or a feeling we get. It's a *decision* we have to make. It's how we respond to God's love – by believing in him and by loving him back. And how can we really love God if we don't love the people he's put into our lives?"

Looking at the girl, Del suddenly felt that she was treading on shaky ground. The invisible wall the child kept around herself had begun to crumble during their conversation, but was now firmly back in place. Del wisely decided not to pursue the subject any further, but made much fuss about getting the cobbler ready so that it would be baked and cooled in time for supper.

21

Wild Things

Del continued to take Mara out for their afternoon learning sessions in the woods. She demonstrated how to obtain safe, drinkable water by using a piece of clear plastic to condense moisture from the ground and have it run off into a container formed from flexible strips of tree bark. Del also explained how the watery sap derived from trees could be a pure source of drinking water, with just a hint of sweetness.

"Unfortunately," she remarked, "it would only be available in the late winter when the sap's rising."

On another day, they covered the finer points of building a shelter out of branches. Mara already had some knowledge on this subject, because her father had taught her similar things on their camping trips. So Del expanded on what the girl knew, showing how to shingle a lean-to snugly with bark and evergreen boughs in such a way that rain would be unable to leak through. Next they constructed a comfortable sort of mattress made up of soft fir tree branches layered a foot deep. The girl tried it out and was surprised at how springy it was, and the woodsy Christmas-tree smell was certainly a delightful bonus.

Del was having a good time showing her young guest the skills she had learned long ago from her mother on their overnight wilderness trips. Her own children had been interested while young, but after they had reached a certain age they couldn't be bothered any more. *Their friends thought I was a bit weird, I suppose.*

Then she sighed. *Good heavens, this child and I have really just been playing around. I no more believe that she could survive for long in the woods by herself than I could fly to the moon. But she hasn't made any move to leave. Maybe one of these days I'll bring up the idea of trying to phone her dad. Lord, just help me buy some time until I figure out how to help her.*

One day while they were in the woods, Mara wandered away from Del and found herself deep in a patch of poison ivy. "Don't move!" shouted the woman, who proceeded to point out the best path for Mara to extricate herself from the dilemma. Then Del searched for her favorite remedy – jewelweed – saying that wherever poison ivy is found, usually jewelweed is growing not far away.

"Ah, I knew it!" she exclaimed, spying the distinctive form of the large, delicate-looking plant, with its spotted orange flowers dangling jewel-like from slender, nodding stems. She pulled off a handful of the greenery, instructing the girl to crush it in her palms and rub the resulting juice on her arms.

"Make sure you cover every bit of skin, and with a little luck you won't get any rash at all. You know," she continued, "jewelweed is nature's pharmacy. It's good not only for rashes, but for stings, bites, sores – even hemorrhoids!"

Del also showed the girl the stands of staghorn sumac growing at the edge of the woods. Del broke off a branch of the sumac and let Mara feel the brown fuzzy covering, like that on a deer's antlers, which gave the plant its name. The soft pith inside, she said, could be poked out with a sharp tool to make the spiles used to collect maple sap in winter.

"And the red sumac berries make a wonderful lemonade-like drink. We'll come back when they're ripe to pick some."

There was always something new to learn out in the woods, but they didn't neglect the garden either. As new flowers bloomed, there were the spent blossoms to be dead-headed, and often whole plants were sheared back to force them to bloom again the same summer. The heavier flowers would frequently bend over and had to be tied, as inconspicuously as possible, to slender stakes. Of course, the watering and weeding were daily chores, but the girl didn't seem to mind the tasks. She often consulted the garden maps to learn the names of the flowers. Del had a way of making it all interesting, telling stories of how she obtained this plant or that one, or how a flower had gotten its unusual name.

Later that week, Del was delighted to see that the daylilies lining the far end of her backyard were sending up tall leafless stalks, loaded with slender green buds showing a blush of coral. She brought out a bowl and picked handfuls of the buds, leaving plenty, however, to develop into the familiar orange flowers. Mara watched but didn't say anything, even after Del had steamed the daylilies, put a pat of butter on the top and set the dish on the table with the rest of their supper.

However, when she saw Del spear some of the buds and lift them to her mouth, the girl could remain silent no longer.

"Really!" she exclaimed. "Why do you eat so many weird things?"

Del smiled but didn't say anything right away, as she was simply enjoying her supper too much. But after she had finished a few mouthfuls, she answered the girl.

"Oh," she said, "what seems strange to one person is perfectly normal to another. Take dandelions, for instance. Very few of us think of dandelions as anything but weeds in our lawns. Yet they were brought over to this country by the early settlers who used the young leaves as salad greens and the cooked roots as vegetables. *And,* they used the yellow flowers to make wine!"

Del attacked a daylily bud with her fork and waved it around in the air while she continued her lecture.

"You can't even imagine how much more nutritious wild plants are, compared to the store-bought stuff we're used to eating. Did you know that dandelions have more beta-carotene than carrots? And more iron than spinach? And loads of other nutrients, too, not to mention their medicinal value. Dandelion tea is one of the most popular herbal remedies for all kinds of ailments."

Del stopped long enough to take another bite, then the girl interrupted her again.

"Don't tell me your family *liked* eating this stuff!"

Del got a guilty look on her face, before admitting, "Well, I didn't always tell them what they were eating. These, for instance," she pointed to the cooked buds, "I called 'oriental vegetables'."

Mara shook her head, but she was smiling. "And they never caught on?"

"Well, once my husband came home from work and demanded to know what smelled funny. 'Like weeds cooking,' he said. I had to admit that I was boiling up some daylily tubers. But, honestly, the roots are quite tasty when prepared like corn!" she said defensively, and Mara couldn't keep from laughing.

"Okay," Del chuckled, "so I didn't fool them. At least not *that* time!"

22

A Different Sort of Meal

On Friday, Del poked her head out the front door, saying, "Hey! I just remembered that I need to go to town today. Want to come with me?"

"Sure," agreed Mara, and muttered under her breath, "at least it's something different to do." She was just finishing mowing the front lawn using an old push-type mower. "Why do I need the gas-powered kind," Del had asked, "when the lawn is so small? Besides, not using gas is better for the environment!" The girl was almost starting to get used to Del's explanations.

Over an early lunch, Del stated that she had nearly forgotten that it was her turn to bring the flowers to decorate the church.

"Other people used to automatically assume that I wouldn't mind bringing flowers all the time. One year I finally insisted that it wasn't fair, that someone else needed to have the *opportunity* to donate some of their own time and labor to the Lord's house. I mean, other people have gardens, too. So what if they're not as extensive as mine! So I set up a rotating schedule where four of us take turns for one weekend each month. And today's my day."

After eating, they went out into the garden carrying a couple of plastic pails with water in the bottom. Del wasn't at all happy that she had forgotten to cut the flowers in the morning.

"The hot afternoon is absolutely the worst time to pick flowers. But I guess we have no choice. Luckily," she said glancing up at the sky, "it's overcast today."

First they cut long stems of red and gold butterfly weed and added white ones to offset the brilliant colors. Next they picked a few lilac-colored pincushion flowers and set them in the buckets, along with delicate, deep-purple spikes of perennial salvia. They filled in with a few other flowers and some variegated foliage from shrubs, and set the pails carefully behind the front seat of the car.

Del drove more slowly on this trip in order not to tip over the flowers. She unlocked the doors of the church and they carried the pails to the maintenance room. They removed the vases from the altar area, dumped the wilting blossoms, scrubbed out the vases and refilled them with fresh water. As the two of them arranged the fresh flowers, Del gave only a few pointers as they worked sided by side. She mentioned the necessity of pulling off all leaves below the water line so they wouldn't rot, but otherwise left the girl pretty much to her own devices.

Mara seemed pleased as she critically examined her finished bouquets.

"Hey, that's really quite good!" exclaimed Del, admiring them. "I think, child, that you have a lot of talent when it comes to flowers."

The girl smiled shyly and helped the woman set the vases on the floor around the altar. They stepped back and double-checked the arrangement, then pulled out the vacuum cleaner and gave the church carpeting a once-over. Del announced that she wanted a few moments to pray before leaving, so Mara wandered through the church building looking more closely at things that had caught her attention the previous Sunday. She ended up behind the altar, looking up at the wall-sized mosaic composed of thousands of tiny tiles. A huge circle of colored tiles radiated outward like a vibrating sun, and in the center of the mosaic was a glittering, gold, long-stemmed cup.

"A chalice," Del explained, coming over to stand next to her. Over the chalice was pictured a flat white disc with a cross on it, and now that Mara was close she could see words arching over and around the large colored circle:

"The Eucharist is that Love which surpasses all love
in Heaven and on earth"

Along the bottom of the circle it read, "St. Bernard of Clairveaux." The girl started to ask a question when Del glanced out the open doors and exclaimed, "Let's hurry along! It's going to rain!"

After locking the church and jumping quickly into the car, Mara was surprised that they turned, not towards Windmill

Gardens, but in the opposite direction, stopping near some stores in a strip mall.

"I need to pick up a few groceries," declared Del. "While I'm doing that, why don't you hop over to that other store and pick up any personal items you need?" Del stuffed a twenty-dollar bill into the girl's hand.

The girl protested, "I can't take your money," saying that she had some of her own.

"You just hold on to your money. You may need it."

Del hoisted herself out of the car, putting an end to the matter. So the girl enjoyed browsing the store aisles, selecting a few items she needed and splurging on a pack of gum. She emerged just as Del came hurrying out of the grocery store with a bulging paper sack. As they started for home, the first raindrops hit, and it turned into a steady downpour by the time they pulled into the garage.

"What a great day to make pizza!" Del exclaimed, setting the bag on the kitchen counter and pulling out a large chunk of mozzarella cheese.

"*Pizza!*" the girl squealed. "We're going to have pizza?"

Del laughed. "Well, it's not my usual fare, but I thought you might be getting a little tired of eating *weeds!* Besides, I haven't had homemade pizza since the last time my son was home."

The woman mixed up the dough and set it to rise while she went off to say her prayers. Mara sat on the floor to play with the kittens. She tried wiggling a straw before their front paws, but they were still a bit young to know enough how to chase it. So she contented herself with picking them up and cuddling them, and watching their babyish attempts to play with each other. When they became tired, she lifted them back into their box, picked up a gardening book and settled down on the living room sofa to read. It was so peaceful with the rain beating against the roof, she eventually dozed off and didn't wake up until Del pulled a large umbrella out of the living room closet.

"Where are you going?" Mara asked, rubbing her bleary eyes. "You're not going out in the woods in *this* weather, are you?"

Del shook her head, saying that she was just going to the garden to pick some fresh basil and oregano for the pizza. "And maybe some green onions would be good, too," adding that it was too early in the season for green peppers. But that was fine with the girl, who wasn't fond of peppers anyway.

Del soon returned, her umbrella leaving trails of water on the floor. She set to work chopping the herbs and asked Mara to get some tomato sauce and mushrooms from the pantry. The girl had learned by now that the pantry was really a large closet in the back room where Del kept all her home-canned jars of tomato sauce, peaches, pears and jellies. She opened the closet door in the rain-darkened room and groped around for the pull string on the overhead light bulb.

What her hand landed on, however, was not a string, but something cool and damp and feeling a bit like human flesh.

"Eeeugh!" she yelled, jumping back and wiping her hand on her jeans.

Del came to see what the problem was. Smiling and shaking her head, she yanked on the light and pulled from the closet shelf a box filled with dirt – and live, growing mushrooms!

"It's just my mushroom garden," she explained kindly to Mara, who was a little embarrassed at her overreaction. "There's nothing like fresh mushrooms any time you want them." Then she added, somewhat unnecessarily to anyone who knew her, "I got it through a mail-order catalog."

"Why don't you pick 'em in the woods like you do everything else?" the girl asked as she cleaned and sliced the mushrooms.

"Well, they're one thing you don't want to fool around with unless you're an expert in mushrooms. There's a lot of poisonous look-alikes out there. Sometimes in the spring I come across a few morels which are easy to identify. And if I'm really lucky, once in a while I'll find a mushroom called a sulphur shelf. It's easy enough to recognize because it grows on trees in the fall and is bright orange."

The dough was soon rolled out, topped with sauce, herbs, mushrooms and cheese, and set to bake in the oven. The smell of it was so enticing that the girl seemed hardly able to wait, and she jumped up to take it out as soon as the timer rang. After they had devoured most of the hot savory pizza, the girl leaned comfortably back in her chair and asked Del how long it had been since her son had been home.

"Oh, he was here for a few days last Christmas. When he was in college, he'd always come home for several weeks during the summer. But since graduating last year, he's got himself a good job and now they've sent him to Germany for a few months." She sighed, saying, "I really do miss him, but what can I do?"

Then Del, without really thinking about it, asked, "What about you? Isn't there anyone that you miss?"

Immediately, she thought, *Oh, maybe I shouldn't have asked that. Lord, help me.*

But, perhaps because of the pizza, the girl was in a more mellow mood and she hardly hesitated before answering, "Yeah. I miss Stephie."

"Stephie?"

"She's my little sister." Mara looked at Del and smiled. "She's almost two, and she's so cute. You should see her…Oh wait, I've got a picture of her!" She went quickly to get her purse and, pulling out her wallet, showed a photo of a smiling toddler with ringlets of golden hair.

"She certainly is cute," Del agreed, wondering, *A sister who's not yet two and a father who left four years ago? Maybe she has a stepfather who she doesn't get along with.* But all she said out loud was, "Do you help take care of her much?"

Mara nodded. "Sometimes it's a pain. But most of the time I don't mind watching her while my mother works. Stephie talks all the time. She calls me 'Mawa' and gives me big bear hugs." Mara was starting to get tears in her eyes, so Del tried distracting her by bringing her attention to another picture that had slipped from her wallet.

"That must be your boyfriend," she said smiling, gently teasing the girl.

Mara lowered her eyes while sliding the boy's photo back in place. "No," she said unconvincingly. "Peter's just a friend." She put her wallet back in her purse and glanced over at Del.

"Pete and I grew up together. We live on the same street and have known each other since we were little. He's been like a solid rock in my life. I can talk to him about anything. Well, almost anything…" she trailed off, looking out the window at the rain. There was a long pause, then in a soft voice she added, "I guess I miss him too."

23

Del's Prayer

Late Sunday morning found them once more barreling down the dirt road towards church. Suddenly Del smacked her forehead with the palm of her hand. .

"Oh, dear!" she cried. "I seem to be forgetting everything lately! It's my turn today to bring Communion after Mass to those who are too old or sick to come to church. Now what are we going to do?"

Del swung the old green boat into the church parking lot and ground to a halt. She switched off the ignition and turned to the girl seated in the roomy passenger seat.

"You're welcome to make the rounds with me if you'd like, but it takes a long time since the old folks want me to sit and visit with them awhile. Or," she continued slowly, thinking while she spoke, "maybe you could go home with Richard and Ann to their farm and I could pick you up there when I'm done."

The girl shrugged her shoulders, looking undecided. Del could see that she was a little nervous about the idea of going anywhere with people she didn't know very well. So she told her to think about it during Mass and they'd decide later.

Setting the problem before the Lord as she prayed for guidance, Del was happy to see that Ann was at church with her husband today. *Ann will be very open to the idea,* she thought, *and Mara would probably be more at ease with her.*

After Mass, Del was quick to point out to anyone who'd listen that Mara had helped arrange the beautiful flowers by the altar. Several people complimented the girl, causing her to smile and blush a little. But it was Del who blushed the most when a tall silvery-haired gentleman came up behind her and landed a kiss on her cheek before she knew what was happening.

"G'morning, Del!" he exclaimed, a smile on his handsome face. "Did you miss me while I was on vacation?"

Del, her dark eyes sparkling, quickly regained her composure and retorted, "Why, George, I didn't even realize you were gone!" *What a lie,* she thought, *but I don't want him taking anything for granted!* The man just laughed, his straight teeth shining white in his tanned face. The others present also smiled, accustomed to the bantering between irrepressible Del and the good-looking widower George.

Del introduced the girl to him, then quickly excused them both as she wanted to catch Richard and Ann before they left. The younger couple was more than happy to invite Mara over. Ann glanced at her watch, saying, "We'll have some lunch. You must be starved by now."

Richard chimed in with a grin, "All you'll get at the old folks' is tea 'n biscuits!"

Mara was probably most persuaded by their little girl, about six years old, who latched on to her hand and jumped up and down excitedly, begging her to come. Del watched them all pile into Richard's blue pickup with its family-sized cab, and waited until it disappeared down the road toward the Spencer farm.

As the last stragglers waved goodbye to Del and pulled out of the parking lot, she closed the doors of the church against the heat of the June day. She went back into the cool interior to wait while Father Mike finished putting away a few things. Then the priest took a gold pyx – a small container for carrying the Eucharist – placed a few consecrated hosts in it and handed it to Del with a smile and a blessing. The woman hurried out to make her Communion visits.

Today's rounds seemed to take an especially long time. It was several hours before Del arrived back at the church to return the pyx to its designated cupboard. Still, before she left for the Spencer farm, she felt drawn to spend at least a few moments before the tabernacle in the quiet church.

She felt so drained as she knelt there and tried to clear her mind. It seemed even more difficult than usual, so she finally just plunged into prayer and laid out all her concerns about her young guest.

I know you know all her problems, Lord, and I'm only guessing. But it seems like she's running away from them instead of trying to face them. I don't know what to do at this point. Are you telling me to "Wait?" I've been trying to do that, but I don't know if I'm hearing you correctly. And sometimes my big mouth *threatens to get me into trouble…*and Del went on and on, because it would never occur to her that her Jesus wasn't interested in every little detail of her life. Everything, big and small, she brought to him and laid at his feet.

Every so often, especially when she was tired and distracted, it would happen that Satan, the Deceiver, would come and whisper in her ear. As she knelt in prayer this day, his voice began to whine, "Why would God listen to you? How can you help anyone else when you don't deserve God's help? Look at all the things you've done. Do you really think God could love *you*?" As the dark thoughts kept tormenting her mind, Del struggled to ignore them but to no avail.

At long last, with wisdom gained from hours of prayer and her habit of emptying everything in her heart before the throne of God, Del took her attention off her own unworthiness. As she refocused her mind on Jesus, the voice faded away and peace returned.

George's affectionate kiss had brought back a flood of memories about her dear husband Joseph, so she brought those also to the Lord. She thanked God for sending Joe to her when she was most in need, and was truly grateful for the good years they had had together. Yet, even after all this time, the aching loneliness was still there. *I miss him so much, Lord.*

But Del didn't dwell in that empty place in her heart for long, as she knew that self-pity would only invite the Deceiver to return. She determinedly turned back to the One who was present there with her.

It is you that I miss the most, my Jesus. I was used to receiving you every day, and now we have Mass only once a week – and it isn't enough! I am so weak, my Lord, I need your presence with me all the time. She sighed inwardly. *But there's nothing I can do about that. So, Jesus, I trust in you.*

Del spent a few more moments in silence before the Lord before leaving and locking up the church. As she drove away, she prayed that Mara had enjoyed her afternoon at the Spencer farm, distracted for a while from her problems.

24

The Spencer Farm

After arriving at the farm after Mass, Mara had helped Ann prepare a simple lunch, setting out bread, sliced meat and some cheese on the table. Ann spooned homemade applesauce, golden-brown with cinnamon and cloves, into a bowl, and little Abby kept up a steady stream of chatter while lining up chocolate chip cookies on a plate.

"I made 'em, didn't I?" Abby asked her mother, who smiled and nodded, agreeing, "Yes. Well, some of them anyway."

Ann turned to Mara. "Abby is such a big help to me, and she's really looking forward to taking care of the new baby." Mara looked at the little girl whose dark curly hair and mischievous eyes resembled her father. She had to suppress a grin as she wondered how this little ball of scattered energy could be of much assistance to anyone.

She looked around the kitchen of the family's farmhouse. The new appliances clearly showed that it had been updated at some point, yet the kitchen still had an old-fashioned charm to it. Since what she had seen of the rest of the house made her wonder how old it was, she asked Ann.

"Oh, this house was built in the early 1900's. It belonged to Richard's grandparents, and when they died they left the whole farm to him. Actually, this is just a portion of the original property. We have only about a hundred sixty acres. My in-laws own all the rest of the land, and their farm backs up to this property."

By now, Richard and their son Sean had come into the house after attending to a few chores, and were washing up in the adjoining utility room. As he dried his hands, Richard said, "It's a good thing my grandfather left me this place. It's awfully hard to break into farmin' with the high cost of land and equipment these days. But most of what we needed was already here, so we're able to make a livin', humble as it is, off this place."

Everyone was seated and Richard said a blessing before passing around the food. Abby, excited about having company for lunch, continually interrupted as she bounced in her seat. In spite of the distraction, Mara managed to catch the story about how Richard's father, with the help of his two younger brothers, ran a dairy farm "on the other side," as he put it.

"Over here, though," he went on, "we have a pretty small operation with a lot fewer cows, and we concentrate on producin' and sellin' the cream. Ann and Sean take care of the chickens and sell the extra eggs. I'm sure the kids'll be happy to show you around after lunch."

Abby jumped up from her seat, delighted to be given the privilege of taking care of their guest, and it took some cajoling on the part of her parents to persuade her to finish her meal. At last they were done, and Ann shooed them all out the door so she could clean up in quiet. Abby grabbed Mara's hand, pulling her toward the chicken coop. Sean, who was auburn-haired and tall for his age and had the quieter personality of his mother, followed behind.

Yet it was Sean who took over the talking once they had reached the enclosed chicken yard. Mara said she was surprised to see chickens that weren't white, as she assumed all chickens were. The boy pointed out to her the different breeds – Rhode Island Reds, Araucanas, Golden Comets and the black-and-white Barred Plymouth Rocks. These last reminded Mara of the paintings she had made in kindergarten by pulling a comb in a wavy pattern through paint on paper. *So many colors,* she thought. *I guess it's not surprising they'd lay such pretty eggs.*

She asked, "Can we go in and get some of their eggs?"

"Oh, no," declared little Abby before her brother had a chance to answer. "You can only gather 'em after supper when the hens get off their nests. Then Mommy has to wash 'em and we put 'em in egg cartons." Mara wondered just how many of the eggs made it intact into the cartons if Abby was helping. The little girl tugged on her hand, leading her on a tour of the large barn and other buildings. They finished by climbing a hill on the far side of the barn where they could look out over the pastures. In the distance Mara could barely make out some brown-and-white cows in a grove of trees.

"Those are Guernseys," said Sean. "There are also a few Jerseys, which you can't see as well in the shade because they're all brown. My grandpa raises Holstein cows, which give *lots* of milk, but we have these kinds 'cuz their milk has so much cream in it. Come on, we'll show you what we do with the milk."

They headed back to the house, stopping long enough to watch the barn kittens for a few minutes. *They're not as cute as Ginger,* thought the girl, *but at least these are old enough to play.* Abby wanted the three of them to stay and play with the kittens, but she trailed reluctantly after her brother and their guest back into the house.

The utility room contained all kinds of equipment that Mara had never seen before. The boy eagerly explained the procedure of pouring fresh milk through a giant stainless steel strainer lined with a paper filter, then dumping it into a machine that had two long spouts protruding like outstretched arms.

"That's the separator. It spins around and the milk comes out here into a container and the cream goes out there into another container. Then we keep the cream cold in this refrigerated vat..."

"'Til the cream man comes!" finished Abby, throwing her arms into the air and dancing a little jig.

"So tell me, Abby," said Mara with a smile, "do your brown cows give you chocolate milk?"

At that the little girl stopped, put her hands on her hips, frowned and scolded her guest.

"Don't be *dericulous*," she said, seriously. Mara laughed and asked Sean what the last machine was used for.

"That's a pasteurizer," he explained, "to heat up the milk that we use for drinking, just hot enough to kill the germs. Any cream we keep for ourselves we pasteurize, too. Hey, maybe you can come over some time and we'll make ice cream!"

Abby got pretty excited at that idea, although it didn't take much to get Abby excited about any idea at all. Ann came into the room at that moment and said she had made some lemonade they all could have outside. Off scooted Abby, followed by her brother. Ann had Mara help her gather together some paper cups and napkins and carry them, together with a pitcher of ice-cold lemonade, outside to where the kids were waiting in the shade of a large tree. Ann set the items on the seat of a white plastic chair, and settled her very pregnant body down in another chair with a sigh of relief.

"Sure is hot in that house," she said, and asked Mara if she'd mind pouring for everyone. It wasn't long before Richard joined them. They tried to visit until, at last, even patient Ann had had enough of her daughter's interruptions and ordered the little girl to go and find something to do. After Abby reluctantly complied, trotting off to play on the tire swing hanging from a branch of a nearby pine tree, Richard turned to their guest. With a twinkle in his eye, he asked, "So! What do you think of our Del?"

Mara's brow furrowed. *What do I think of her? She's... she's...* Since the teenager seemed at a loss for words, Richard laughed loudly.

"That's okay, we don't know how to describe her either! And have you gotten used to eating weed casseroles yet?"

The girl wrinkled her nose and declared, "I don't know if I ever will!"

Yet she didn't want to sound as if she was complaining about her generous host, so she simply added, "Del seems very nice."

Both Richard and Ann smiled and agreed that their friend Del was probably one of the kindest people they knew.

"When she gets a phone call from someone needing something, off she goes. And sometimes the older folks will call her – in the evenings, you might have noticed, because they know she won't be out in the garden then– just to talk with her because they're lonely. And she always listens. Says that God listens to her whenever she wants to talk, so she can certainly listen to others."

Richard stopped for a moment, then continued in a more serious tone, "It was Del who got me to start going to church every week. I tried telling her there was too much to do on the farm, but she wouldn't let me off the hook. She kept asking me what in my life was more important than God. Believe me, that was a tough question to answer! And she got after me about praying. I told her I *did* pray but not on a regular basis, and she said that wasn't good enough. She said if I didn't have a *plan* to pray, I wouldn't remember to pray. Of course, she was right," Richard admitted ruefully, rubbing his chin.

Meanwhile, Mara was thinking, *He's just like Del, always telling me more than I wanted to know!* Richard, who definitely liked to talk, didn't notice the discomfiture of the girl and started to say something else. But just then the old green boat pulled into the driveway in a cloud of dust.

25

Back to Nature

Del apologized for being so late, and handed Ann a glass jar of golden honey. "It's from Bob Burwood's bees," she said. "He was there visiting his mother when I brought her Communion. He gave me two jars, but I told him he owed me lots more than that 'cause his bees were getting all their nectar from my garden!"

She laughed as heartily as always, although there was a haze of fatigue over her perspiring face. Ann offered to make her a sandwich but Del declined graciously, explaining that the last people she had visited insisted she stay for lunch after she gave them Communion.

"But a glass of that lemonade would really hit the spot," she declared, then looked over at Richard.

"I'm afraid Esther Briggs isn't doing well at all," she said, knowing that her neighbor was fond of the elderly woman. "Her daughter has come up to stay with her. When I brought Esther Communion today, I learned from Alice that she isn't likely to last much longer. Still, sick as she is, she was ever so sweet, thanking me over and over again for bringing Jesus to her."

Del paused for a moment before saying, "You know, Esther was the first person to visit me when we moved here. I always called her when I had any questions about raising the children. She was like a second mother to me and a grandmother to my kids." Del stopped to take a sip of the cold lemonade in order to regain her composure, adding, "Alice said she'll let me know if her mom takes a turn for the worse."

Del sighed, then turned toward Mara, asking, "Did you get a tour of the farm?"

The girl nodded and asked Del a question of her own.

"When did you move here?"

"Well, after Joe and I got married, we lived in the city for a few years. But at one point we started to talk about moving out to the country where the kids would have more space to grow up. I guess what really clinched it," Del said, smiling at the memory, "was when we took our children to see one of those 'living nativities' they have at Christmastime. You know, where they use real people and real animals? My younger son insisted we go pet the 'camel', and it *mooed* at us!" She chuckled.

"I told Joey we needed to get our kids back in touch with nature. We didn't want the responsibility of having a farm, but we did want to be closer to animals and the woods. And like I told you before, when we saw the windmill we said, 'That's it!'" Del stopped her narrative and glanced at her watch. "Speaking of the windmill, we really need to get back home!"

After many thank you's, along with multiple hugs and squeezes from Abby, the two headed up the road to Windmill Gardens. Pulling the old car carefully into the garage, Del turned off the ignition and asked Mara, "How do you like little Abby?"

"Oh, she's really cute," Mara replied quickly. "And smart! But she is rather, uh…*active,* isn't she?"

Del pulled her weary body out of the car. The day was really humid and it seemed to her like every joint ached.

"Yes, our Abby is certainly a busy girl, and it can wear on you sometimes," she said, although one could see that she dearly loved the child. "When I babysit for her and Sean, I have a hard time keeping up with her. Or getting a word in edgewise," she added. She opened the door and entered the house, totally oblivious to the fact that when she and Richard got together, it was mighty difficult for anyone else to get a word in edgewise, either.

As she rummaged through the refrigerator for some leftovers to reheat for an easy supper, her muffled voice floated out on a cloud of chilled air.

"A long time ago when my kids were young their behavior was like Abby's. There were times I thought they were going to drive me crazy." She pulled out some soup and dumped it into a saucepan to warm.

"After a lot of prayer and research, I finally decided we were all going to eat more naturally. You know, eliminate additives in our food – like artificial colors and preservatives. We really did notice a difference. Our kids were a lot calmer and they didn't get sick nearly as much. I've tried to tell Ann about it to help Abby, but I guess she's got her hands full right now."

Then, in an abrupt change of subject that was so typical of Del, she exclaimed, "Hey! Let's make some fry bread to go with the soup!"

"Fry bread? What's *that*?" asked Mara cautiously, sounding as if she hoped there were no surprises, like plant roots, in it – or heaven forbid, something even worse. Del didn't answer but took out a bowl and put into it a heaping handful of flour.

"Now we'll add baking powder and a pinch of salt. Here, why don't you cut in this shortening? Then you can mix in some water and I'll get the oil heating up to fry it in."

While Del dropped spoonfuls of batter into the hot oil, Mara stirred the soup and set the table. Soon they were enjoying the crispy hot bread with their meal. Del explained that her mother used to make fry bread all the time.

"In fact, by leaving out the shortening you have a basic bread that's popular with campers. You wrap the dough around a clean stick and hold it over a campfire until it's cooked through."

They both ate until they were nearly full, saving just enough room for the cookies that Ann had sent home with them. Mara suddenly remembered Del's earlier words. She asked, "So what's wrong with the colors and preservatives in food?"

"Well, most people don't know this, but they are made from petroleum, which is certainly not food. And a lot of other chemicals besides. Some people are really sensitive to them. And it makes sense to me since, for most of human history, we ate our food as nature intended it to be." For some reason the thought of eating bugs popped into Mara's head, but surely that wasn't what Del meant.

"It's only been in this last century or so that we've drastically altered our food, like adding chemicals to just about everything we eat. It's not surprising that some people, especially children whose bodies are more vulnerable to everything, react in negative ways to this processed stuff we call food."

Del paused to take a breath, looking out the window at the evening garden with the lengthening shadows creeping slowly across. She continued thoughtfully, "That's one reason I started going out into the woods again to get some of our food, which I really hadn't done since my mother died. Wild food is unprocessed and high in nutrition. And it's free for the taking!

"So!" Del said, winking at the girl. "Tomorrow afternoon it's back to our wilding!"

26

The Rosary

The next morning, after they had weeded and watered the vegetable plots, Del introduced Mara to the many herbs scattered throughout the gardens. Some, like oregano and the tall, graceful dill, were growing alongside the vegetables. Others, including chamomile with its fuzzy gray-green foliage and tiny buttons of yellow blossoms, looked right at home with the ornamental flowers. And borage's star-like blue flowers towered over the strawberry garden, where its strong scent helped to protect the berries from insects.

Del beckoned the girl over to a smaller garden tucked among the others.

"I have some of my tea plants grouped together here. That small shrub in the back is lemon verbena, and there's yarrow and lemon balm. And here," she indicated clay pots scattered around in the herb garden, "are different kinds of peppermint."

Of course, Mara questioned her why the mints were growing in pots instead of in the ground. Del replied, "Because they're pushy, that's why! Give 'em an inch of ground and they'll take a mile! Here, smell these." She picked leaves from several of the plants and the girl was surprised to discover the different scents of the varieties of mint. Amazingly, some smelled a little like chocolate, others like orange or apple.

"All the mints, whatever their scents, can easily be identified by their square stems," the woman explained. "Have you ever had fresh peppermint tea? Boy, it's so-o-o much better than the store-bought stuff!"

She continued to identify the various herbs and how she dried many of them to sell at the farmer's market.

"The use of herbs has skyrocketed in recent years. People have gotten tired of the side effects of drugs and are looking for more natural remedies. Tell you what, let's pick this peppermint and brew some tea to have with our lunch today. Mint is great for digestion!"

Mara said nothing, but as they went into the house perhaps she was thinking that some of Del's unique recipes needed a little help being digested.

After the lunch dishes were cleaned up, the woman headed to the living room as always for her afternoon prayer time. But this day Mara followed her. She seemed a bit restless and bored, so maybe that was what prompted her question. As she saw Del settle herself back into her easy chair, put up her feet and pick up her rosary, she suddenly asked, "What are those beads for, anyway?"

Del put her feet down and sat up. If she was annoyed at having her quiet time with the Lord interrupted, she didn't show it. She just smiled at the girl and held up the circular string of shiny black beads with a cross dangling from it.

"Well," she began, "this is what we call a 'rosary.' It helps us to keep track of the prayers that we're saying. This rosary here has plastic beads and is really inexpensive, but in my bedroom I have one my mother gave me which has crystal beads and a metal chain. Of course, that one has a lot of sentimental value to me, but this one works just fine too. Here, I'll show you how the Rosary prayers are said."

Del spent the next few minutes explaining how each set of ten beads, or "decade," is made up of ten "Hail Mary" prayers. Each decade is preceded by the Lord's Prayer, which she called an "Our Father," and ends with a simple but profound prayer of praise: "Glory be to the Father and to the Son and to the Holy Spirit, as it was in the beginning, is now and ever shall be, world without end. Amen."

"And while praying each decade," she said, "you meditate on an episode in the life of Christ and his mother. For instance, you think about what it was like in the stable the night Jesus was born. Or maybe in the garden on the morning of his resurrection."

"You've got to be kidding!" was Mara's reaction. "You're supposed to say prayers while thinking about something else?"

Del just laughed. "Don't tell me you never did two things at once! Like doing homework and listening to the radio – or watching TV?"

With a small smile, the girl admitted, "Well ...maybe sometimes."

Del continued, "The Rosary actually engages two levels of our brain at once, so by meditating while saying the prayers we can be more focused…"

"So how," Mara interrupted, obviously not focused herself, "did this Rosary get started?"

Del explained that, even in the earliest days of the Christian church, people would set aside a certain span of time each day for prayer, and it soon became a custom to keep track of one's prayers by using small stones. Later on, to make them easier to use, the stones or some beads were strung on rope, or the rope itself was knotted to use for counting. Eventually the prayers were grouped into the familiar decades and meditations that millions of people all over the world pray today. ·

"But why," the girl persisted, "don't you just pray to God in your own words?"

"Good question!" declared Del, her animated dark eyes crinkling at the corners. "Certainly, any time you want you can pray to God in your own words. In fact, the Bible does tell us to 'Pray always!' I myself try to pray while I'm working or doing most anything. But you know what I've found?"

She paused for a moment and her thoughts seemed to go off in the distance somewhere. Then she brought her gaze back to the girl's face and continued in a quieter, more reflective voice.

"What I've discovered is that most of the time – whether I'm praying for guidance or whatever, or for other people and their needs, or even for really big things like peace in the world – all these prayers are asking Jesus to come into my world, to heal or forgive or help in some way. I've noticed that even when I'm praising God, it seems somehow to involve the world as I know it.

"And," she added quickly, "there's nothing wrong with that! Jesus is certainly present in our world and wants us to speak to him as naturally as I'm speaking to you! But, you know, when I meditate on the Rosary, for a little while I go into Jesus' world and spend time just being with him. It's like being there when he was in the manger – or on the cross. Praying the Rosary helps me feel as if I'm gazing upon his face, along with his mother who loved him so much. I know that when I spend time with Jesus it's easier for me to act in loving ways like he…"

The girl again interrupted, rather impatiently. "That's really weird! Jesus lived a long time ago. How can you spend time in his world?"

But Del gently pointed out that since Jesus is truly God, he has no confines of time and space. Therefore, in our prayers we can be with him as surely as if we had lived two thousand years ago.

Mara, still rather impatient, asked the woman, "But why repeat the same prayers over and over again?"

For someone who says she doesn't believe in God, she sure has a lot of questions! But Del really didn't mind, since there were few topics so dear to her as her beloved Lord. With a big smile on her face, she answered, "Well, what's wrong with that? People repeat things all the time that mean a lot to them. Like the Pledge of Allegiance. Or favorite songs or poems.

"And who'd ever get tired of hearing the words 'I love you' said over and over to them, as long as they're said with meaning? Most of the words in the 'Hail Mary' come right out of the Bible, and the 'Our Father' is in the words of Jesus himself. How could any prayers I make up be any better than his own words?

"Besides," Del said with a grin, "did you know that Jesus repeated prayers? For sure, since he was a devout Jew, he must have prayed the Psalms over and over again, since that's what the Jewish people did."

Mara shrugged and got up to go to the kitchen where the kittens were starting to jump from their box. Over her shoulder she tossed a parting shot, "Seems kinda boring to me."

Del opened her mouth to respond to the rude remark, then she simply bit her tongue, leaned her head back and closed her tired eyes. *Boring? I guess when I was her age, prayer seemed boring to me, too.*

And, Del admitted to herself, *it can still be a struggle. Maybe I should tell her that it's not the words you say, but the relationship you have with God that gives meaning to prayer.*

In spite of Del's good intentions, she never did get around to finishing this particular conversation with the girl. However, some of the things they talked about must have been swimming around in Mara's mind, because several days later she herself returned to the subject.

27

Forgive Us Our Trespasses

The late afternoon sun was partially hidden by the large swirls of clouds which drifted slowly across the hazy blue sky. That made the day seem not as unbearably hot for the two people crossing a large clearing on the far side of the woods. Except for a few pockets of white daisies and the delicate flowers of Queen Anne's Lace, most of the meadow was blanketed in a sea of blue chicory blossoms. Here and there the brown seedpods of yellow dock plants poked up. They brought a smile to the face of the woman who remembered playing with the seeds as a small child, pretending they were "coffee."

At that time I didn't realize how much real food was around me, Del thought. She was grateful to her mother for giving her the knowledge which she was now trying to impart to her young friend.

Del was nearly finished gathering greens for the evening's meal. She had already gotten some tender shoots of pokeweed which she planned to steam and serve with fresh farm butter, and now was on the lookout for salad fixings. Tall bush-like lamb's quarters were everywhere and she gathered handfuls of their small silvery-backed leaves. As she and Mara re-entered the woods, she picked some twining greenbriers. Then she finished off with plenty of wood sorrel as they followed the path through the meadow and into the garden.

Near the workshop, the woman stopped at one of the smaller gardens which had not yet been weeded. From under the flowers she pulled up a handful of succulent purslane to add to their dinner salad. She popped a few of the round leaves into her mouth and offered some to Mara. Although the girl was hesitant as usual to try it, she finally bit into one and decided that it wasn't too bad after all. In fact, she even seemed to like it.

All of a sudden the girl broached the topic that had been on her mind for awhile.

"Do you remember," she asked, looking under the flowers for more of the tasty weed, "a few days ago when you were talking to me about the Rosary?"

Del answered in the affirmative and waited for the girl to continue.

Mara nibbled on a couple of purslane leaves and said slowly, "Well, I was thinking about the Lord's Prayer. You know, the part that goes, 'Forgive us our trespasses as we forgive those who trespass against us.' Just what do those words really mean?"

Del was unsure exactly what to say, but that had never stopped her before. Asking the Holy Spirit to enlighten her, she replied with a question of her own.

"Well, what do *you* think they mean?"

The girl seemed a bit reluctant to answer, but finally said, "It sounds as if God won't forgive us if we don't forgive others."

This time Del didn't say anything, so the girl went on, "But what if someone does something awful, I mean, *really* bad, to another person? How can that other person be expected to forgive them?"

The girl didn't look at Del but kept her head down as if she was interested in the flowers at her feet. Quietly Del took a deep breath and then seemed to change the subject.

"Child, do you see this workshop here? Remember how I told you that my husband built it? One of the things he had to do before it was finished was to run electricity from the house out to it. To do that, he had to dig a trench through the backyard – that was before the garden was as big as it is now – and lay down some conduit. Do you know what conduit is?"

The girl looked at Del and shook her head, a bit puzzled at this turn of conversation.

"Conduit is sort of a pipe that you run the electric wiring through. I guess, to protect it from moisture or maybe animals chewing it. Or from a certain gardener we both know, who would probably cut through it with a shovel!"

She smiled and continued, "Well, my husband was never one to buy anything he could get for free. So when a friend of his gave him some old conduit he had lying around, Joe was more than happy to take it. There was only one problem. It had been outside on the ground for ages and was all stopped up with mud."

Del was getting warm standing there in the sun, so she tried to bring her story to the point.

"Holding on to unforgiveness only hurts ourselves in the long run. We become like that stopped-up conduit, unable to let God's 'electricity' – his love and grace – flow through us. We can't fully receive God's blessings and we can't be instruments of his love to others. When we *do* forgive, it's like when Joe took a long wooden dowel and poked out that mud."

Del cocked her head to one side, and with a grin added, "You could say that forgiving makes us like conduit – holy conduit!"

Mara almost smiled, but then her face clouded over.

"So, what if you don't *feel* like forgiving someone?"

A look of sadness came over Del's face, and she gazed at the top of the trees beyond the garden as she replied quietly, "Child, forgiveness isn't a feeling. It's a decision you make. And sometimes you have to make that decision over and over again on a daily basis."

She brought her eyes back to the girl and said in a brisker voice, "I don't think anyone can truly forgive a deep hurt without the help of God. Come on, let's go in the house. I want to show you something."

In the kitchen Del deposited her day's bounty on the counter. Then she went to her bedroom, opened the door and invited the girl to follow her.

The room was bright with rays of sunshine slanting in through the white lace curtains in the double window. The bed had a multi-colored quilt thrown over it and there was an oval rag rug on the varnished wood floor. It was no surprise that there were plenty of books in this room also, stacked none too neatly on the bookshelves and nightstand, and even a few lying open, spine side up, on the bed itself.

There were many pictures on the bedroom walls, and Del led her over to a grouping next to the windows. She took down a photo in a plain oak frame.

"This is my daughter Kat."

She showed it to Mara, who found herself looking at what seemed to be a younger version of Del. The young woman, a teenager actually, had straight black hair pulled back from a smiling face. Her lovely olive skin set off a pair of sparkling dark eyes.

The girl looked up from the portrait and asked, "You named your daughter 'Cat'? C-A-T?"

"No, no," Del smiled. "*Kat* with a 'K.' It's short for Kateri. You see, my mother converted to Catholicism when she married my father, and she loved her new-found faith. She was especially devoted to the memory of a young native girl who had died many centuries ago near Montreal, Canada. This girl was honored by the Church because she loved Jesus, and because of her holy life. Her name was Kateri Tekakwitha, and she was part Algonquin and part Mohawk. I remembered how much my mother talked about Kateri, and I wanted to name my daughter for her."

"How old is your daughter now?"

Del hung the picture back on the wall and stared at it, answering softly, "This was her senior photo. She never got to graduate from high school."

The woman's eyes filled with tears but she continued with her explanation.

"Kat went to stay overnight with her friend Julie, who was in her first year of college. During the night, some guys broke into the house where Julie lived off campus. They were looking for money for drugs. In fact, they were so high at the time they didn't even realize they had killed the girls."

Mara was silent, trying to digest the horror of what Del was telling her. All she finally said was, "Were they ever caught?"

"Yes," said Del, "and they're both in prison now." She sighed, trying to get hold of her emotions, and turned to Mara.

"Did you see the flowers on my mailbox? Kat painted those for me. She had plans to study art in college and be an elementary art teacher. I tell you, child, I've had to do a lot of forgiving these past eight years, or it would have eaten me alive. Even now it's one day at a time."

The girl didn't seem to know what else to say, so she pointed to another picture on the wall.

"Is that your husband and you?"

"Yep, that's us," Del replied. "That was on our twentieth anniversary. He only lived another four years after that. He got lung cancer from all the years he worked in a cabinet-making factory. But how he loved working with wood! In his spare time he was always building things. He made all the bookshelves in this house." Del glanced around the room.

There was also a portrait of a man and a woman with two small children that Mara asked about next.

"Oh, that's my older son, Robert, and his wife, Emily. And those are my two granddaughters, Susan and Theresa."

Del smiled broadly, although tears still shone in her eyes. "They live in Colorado so I don't have a chance to see them much, but I talk to them on the phone when I can.

"And this," she said, laying a hand on the frame of the last picture, "is John, my younger son, the one I told you about who's in Germany right now."

Mara looked at the serious face of a brown-haired young man who resembled his mother the least of all. This must be his high-school photo, as he would probably be in his early twenties now. There was also a corkboard nearby on the wall, and Del showed the girl snapshots pinned to it of cousins and various other relatives.

Leaving the bedroom, Del happened to notice the calendar hanging next to the doorway, and she stopped to look more closely at it.

"Goodness, child!" she exclaimed. "It's almost July already! On the first Saturday of every month Richard and I always make a trip to the city. You're more than welcome to come along. Usually Ann goes too with the children, but as she gets closer to her due date she hasn't felt up to it."

She explained, "We have a booth together at the farmer's market there, and while we're in the city we pick up some things we can't get in town. Do you think you'd like to go?"

What a silly question! Mara eagerly said she'd love to, meaning, of course, that anything would be a break in the day-to-day monotony of life in this house. Therefore, early on Saturday morning she was up and ready to go when Richard pulled into the driveway in his pickup.

28

Into the City

It was at least an hour's drive to the city from Windmill Gardens. Mara rode in the back seat of the pickup's cab with young Sean, listening to Richard and Del carrying on a conversation in the front. *The two of them hardly ever take a breath,* she thought, although earlier she had managed to get in a quick question for Richard.

"What do you have in those coolers in the back of the truck?"

Richard glanced in his rear-view mirror at her and answered amiably, "Cream, eggs, milk, stuff like that. Normally the store in town takes my surplus. But on our first Saturday trip I bring everythin' I have to the market. Ann also makes crafts which are in the cardboard box back there. And the wooden crate has some tools I want to sell that I picked up at auction."

Del turned partway around in her seat and continued the explanation. "Usually I have things to sell, too, but summer is my slow time. All I brought today are jars of jelly I made last winter. But before long I'll have dried flowers and herbs.

"Do you remember all the wild grapevines I showed you on one of our trips out to the woods? Well, I gather the vines in the fall and bring them to Ann who makes them into wreaths. Then she uses some of my dried flowers to decorate the wreaths and we sell them at the market."

Del smiled at Richard. "She does a terrific job. They always sell pretty well, don't they?"

Then she addressed the girl again. "Also, in the spring I dig up and bring along all the thinnings from my perennials."

Wow! thought the girl. *That's quite an assortment – eggs and milk, tools and crafts and plants! Well, I've never been to a farmer's market before. Maybe that's the way it's done.*

After that she had settled back in her seat, looking out the window at things of interest that Sean would shyly point out to her. Del and Richard discussed the tomato-growing competition in the community. Although informal and having no official sanction, nevertheless the contest seemed to engage anyone who had a few square feet of ground in which to put a plant. Del boasted that her biggest tomato on her prize plant was almost orange, but Richard claimed that he had heard about another gardener with tomatoes already turning red. A bit disappointed, Del changed the subject to old Mrs. Briggs, with an update on her worsening condition.

Almost before the girl realized it, they had entered the city and were driving down the narrow streets looking for a parking spot near the market. Richard finally gave up hope of finding a convenient one and let his passengers out near the entrance. Hopping out, he unloaded everything onto a wheeled cart that was provided by the management. He went to park while the other three pushed and pulled the cart. They were halfway through the crowded market before he caught up to them.

Mara and Sean were really enjoying the bustle of activity in the large, open-sided building. After they had helped unpack the items and set up the display, the older folks shooed them off to have a look around. The combination of sights, sounds and smells was incredible. The girl had never been anywhere quite like it. She bought hot baked pretzels for the two of them to munch on as they wandered around. At one booth they stopped to pet some fuzzy kittens for sale, and at another watched baby goats – "kids," Sean corrected her – butting their heads together inside a fenced pen. By the time they had gotten back to their own spot, nearly half of the items they'd brought had already been sold and Del was going around greeting the nearby vendors. It was nearly noon when she finally returned with a big smile on her face.

"Hey, Mara!" she exclaimed. "The boys can handle the booth for awhile. I'm going over to Mass at the cathedral and then getting some lunch. Do you want to come with me or stay here?"

Mass on a Saturday? But since lunch was mentioned, Mara elected to go with Del. They left the bustle of the busy market and started walking through what was obviously a poorer section of the city, attested to by the broken windows and graffiti. Del seemed oblivious to her surroundings as she hurried along for the next several blocks.

The cathedral was a beautiful building, but near it garbage littered the streets and groups of aimless young people hung out in front of run-down stores. Entering the cool, dim interior of the church, Mara was struck by the tangible silence. Next she noticed the scent of hundreds of flickering candles and the awesome stained glass windows shining like gems in the darkness.

During Mass the girl looked around her at the couple dozen people in attendance and at the windows, statues and paintings. *This is certainly different from Del's church,* she thought at first. But after listening to the priest's talk, and hearing the prayers and Scripture readings, she decided that it wasn't so different after all. What was it Del had told her? Something about the meaning of the word "catholic."

Oh yeah, it means "universal." Its teachings are the same all over the world, even though some of the customs vary from place to place. The priest in this church was an older man who took his time. *No hurrying through here,* she thought, struck by the reverent singing.

She closed her eyes and her breathing slowed with the quiet rhythm of the Mass, and all at once a sense of peace flooded over her. *Like the peace I sometimes feel in Del's garden,* she reflected. *Almost as if God might actually be near. Maybe I should try praying, as Del says so often.*

So the girl really, truly made an attempt to pray. But before long her mind slid into the past, when she went to church with her parents in that much happier time of her childhood. Then her thoughts, becoming more troubled by the minute, led to the memory of leaving home on that night – *could it be almost a month ago?* – when she had hurriedly yanked on some clothes and stuffed her purse into her backpack. She had almost slipped out the front door when she noticed a wallet on the hall table. After removing a credit card from it, she quickly replaced the wallet before easing the door shut behind her. With no destination in mind she had run just as far and as fast as she could, until that man – *that creepy guy!* – offered to give her a ride. *And then I had to run again!* Against her will a tear squeezed out from under closed lids.

Pray, Mara, pray, came to mind, but she was having a hard time getting past the depression that suddenly gripped her. *What was it Del told me just last night? "Take one day at a time,"* she said. *"Things usually have a way of working themselves out if*

*we just trust in God." But I don't see how anything in this
situation is going to work out! I can't go home, and if my dad has
moved I have nowhere else to go!*

Many times at night she'd dream about a heavy, dark,
foul-smelling blanket lying across her face, almost smothering her,
and she would wake up in a panic, her heart racing. She never told
Del about these nightmares, and remembering them now made her
squeeze her eyes more tightly shut to block out the awful thoughts.

She didn't realize that Del was glancing over at her,
concerned about the emotions playing across the girl's face, or that
the woman immediately turned to God to ask for comfort, hope
and help for Mara. All she knew was that she was a bit startled
when Del put a hand on her arm to tell her Mass was over. Mara
followed Del from the cathedral out onto the marble steps where
the woman asked her kindly if she was all right. The girl nodded,
pretending that the sudden brightness of the sunlight was what was
bothering her eyes. Del spied a fast food restaurant across the
street and suggested they have a bite to eat.

In spite of her feelings the girl's face lit up – *hamburger
and fries!* – and it wasn't long until they had eaten their fill and
were laughing over some silly little thing. On the way back to the
market, Mara amused herself by looking in the store windows. All
of a sudden she became aware that Del seemed to be stooping
down, then stopping and stooping again.

"What are you doing?" demanded the girl, and Del
answered, "Why, I'm picking up trash, of course."

"Why are you doing that? There's so much around here,
what you pick up isn't going to make a difference!"

"That's all right," responded Del mildly. "Every little bit
helps. I always like to leave God's world a little cleaner wherever
I go. Just think if everyone did the same!"

But now the problem was, there didn't seem to be a trash
can anywhere in sight. *Oh, you've got to be kidding!* Mara rolled
her eyes. *She's actually going to carry the trash along with her!*

She began to walk a little faster so it wouldn't look to
anyone else as if she was actually *with* the trash-carrying woman.
She had gotten a bit ahead of Del when, unexpectedly, she heard
from behind her a *thud,* a grunt and then the sound of running
footsteps.

She spun on her heel and saw the last of a teenage boy as
he quickly disappeared down the street. Del stood with her back to

the girl, purse dangling from one hand and the other hand on her hip.

"What happened?" asked Mara, concern in her voice as she hurried back to where the woman stood glaring.

"Why, that young man tried to steal my purse!" Del was outraged.

"What did you do?"

"I whacked him!" Del exclaimed, and she started to walk once again with Mara, the trash lying forgotten on the sidewalk behind her. Then she chuckled.

"And he looked just as surprised as my horse did when I whacked *him!*"

"What horse?"

"The horse I had when I was growing up. One day I was walking through the corral and he was following me looking for a handout. All of a sudden he took it into his head to nip me on my side. Without thinking I spun around and whacked him hard with the back of my hand. Boy, did *he* ever look surprised! Just like that boy." And she chuckled again.

Mara decided that it wasn't safe to let Del walk alone in the city, so she stuck closely by her side until they approached the farmer's market. Then she asked, "Aren't you going to report the attempted purse-snatching?"

Del furrowed her brow. "Well, I hadn't actually thought about it."

"You know, you really should! He might do the same thing to some other lady."

Del sighed. "All right! You're right and that's right! Go on into the market and look for Richard and Sean and I'll hop over to the police station."

Mara was indignant. "By *yourself?*" she asked, as if she thought that she would be a great deal of protection for the woman.

Del tried to suppress a smile.

"Don't worry, it's close by. See? There's the police station, that building with the red roof right over there. Go on in. I'll be fine," she reassured the girl. "Besides, my guardian angel is right here by me."

She waited until Mara disappeared into the crowded market, then turned and headed down the street.

29

Writing in the Sky

As she walked to the police station, Del didn't mind the few minutes alone as it gave her another chance to talk over her concerns with the Lord. Anyone glancing at her might have noticed that she looked distracted, but wouldn't have guessed the interior struggle she was having trying to discern what she should do about the girl. She kept telling God that it was all in his hands, but she would immediately take charge again. Then she would realize how silly it was to apply her own limited wisdom and she would again give the problem back to the limitless God. At least for a few minutes.

Del stopped often to pick up litter and had collected quite a handful, when she suddenly collected her scattered thoughts and burst out in frustration, "Okay, Lord, I guess I'm not able to hear what you're telling me! You'll just have to write it in the sky or something!"

Then, as she continued on her self-imposed mission to clean up this part of the city, for some reason she looked up at the blue cloudless sky and was startled to see a letter forming near the horizon. She stopped walking and stared in disbelief, her mouth slack and her eyes wide open behind her glasses, waiting in utter amazement for what the Lord wanted to tell her.

The first letter, seemingly composed of fluffy white clouds, was finished. It was a "P," and a second letter was starting to take shape.

P? Are you telling me to pray more? Or is it a P for patience?

The second letter was looking like an "F" – no, an "E."

"P-E..." *People? Person?* Or *perhaps* she was to have *peace* in her heart?

The third letter was another "P" and Del was getting more puzzled by the moment. *Pep? Well, I could certainly use a little more of that!*

As she waited as still as a statue for the rest of the message, she was vaguely aware of others starting to gather in groups along the street where they pointed at the sky. When the last two letters were finished, Del was astounded to see written in the heavens the name of a popular soft drink. She couldn't make any sense of it at all until she heard people murmuring about "skywriting" and "air show today" over at a nearby airfield. Then she squinted her eyes and could just make out a tiny glint that was an airplane at the tail end of the last letter.

At that, Del laughed out loud at herself for being taken in by nothing more than a grandiose advertising gimmick. A bit embarrassed, she hurried along on her errand to the police station.

You win, my Jesus, I'll give my problems over to you. If I'm so darn gullible, who knows what foolishness I could come up with next!

Back at the farmer's market, the humorous incident was soon forgotten as the four of them packed up the unsold items. Richard sprinted for the pickup so they could load up quickly. Before leaving the city, they made a stop at a bulk-foods store where they purchased some needed items.

"I'm lucky," said Del, watching Richard hoist a large brown paper sack of flour into the bed of the truck, "it's not raining, or I'd have twenty-five pounds of paste!"

They loaded the rest of the shopping bags and said a tired farewell to the city as they quickly left it behind. The two in the front seat were much quieter on the way home, so Mara used the opportunity to ask Del a few questions that had been on her mind. One in particular had to do with the cathedral where they had attended Mass earlier that day.

"That neighborhood is so poor," the girl said. "Wouldn't it be better if all the money it took to build the cathedral was just given to the poor people?"

Because of her weariness, Del took an extra-long time to shift around so she could look back at the girl while answering.

"Well," she said. "I have to admit that at one time in my life I thought that would certainly be the sensible thing to do. *And* the charitable thing. But now I'm not so sure, and this is why. The Catholic Church has built lots of cathedrals, sure enough. But throughout its nearly two thousand years, it's also built many, many hospitals, schools and orphanages – often in the very poorest communities – and then sends priests, nuns and lots of others to work among those who live in poverty. There's no other charity or religious organization in the entire world which has given nearly as much to help the poor as the Catholic Church."

Del paused to take a breath and Richard grinned. He himself had been in similar arguments with Del. Maybe if she didn't read so darned much he could win a point with her once in awhile!

The woman continued, "Now, what if that beautiful church wasn't there? For over fifty years it's been a little spot of heaven on earth for people in the neighborhood. The cathedral beckons them in, to come and rest from their burdens awhile, to spend some time with their Savior. Rich or poor or in-between, *everyone* is welcome there. What other place can you say that about?"

The girl had no other questions, so there was silence in the cab for a few minutes. All of a sudden Richard burst out with his own question.

"Hey, what are you guys doin' this Tuesday? It's the Fourth of July, you know. Ann and I were plannin' a little picnic and we'd like both of you to come and liven it up. How about two o'clock?"

Del glanced again at Mara, who shrugged her shoulders, so the woman smiled at her neighbor and agreed. They spent the rest of the trip back to Windmill Gardens discussing what kind of food she could contribute to the get-together. With a broad smile, Richard insisted that whatever she brought couldn't have any *weeds* in it. Del retorted that he was fortunate that she was such a good cook that she could hide her *wild foods* in any dish and he'd never even notice. In the back seat, Mara and Sean grinned at each other, shaking their heads. It would certainly be an interesting picnic.

30

Mercy and Forgiveness

The next morning, a Sunday at the very beginning of July, was bright with sunshine and already hot and humid. Del was in the garden watering the thirstiest of the plants, most particularly her beloved hydrangeas growing at the corner of the house near the gate. She had them heavily mulched, but they still required generous drinks of water so that the leaves wouldn't wilt. The bushes were covered with multitudes of globe-shaped flowerheads, at the present greenish-white but beginning to show slight hints of the heavenly blue they would turn in a few short weeks. These large blooms would hang on all the way until autumn when they'd turn green again, tinted with varying shades of purple and maroon. Then she would dry the lovely flowers and sell huge bouquets of them to her customers at the farmer's market.

But she wasn't thinking about her hydrangeas as she kept a stream of water trained at their roots. Many thoughts and prayers crossed her mind while she went about her watering chores until, finished at last, she went in to awaken her young guest in order to get ready for Mass. Del was a little surprised that Mara was still willing to go to church with her, considering that the girl didn't seem to be much of a morning person. She would roll out of bed most days about ten o'clock and often skipped breakfast.

Maybe, Del mused to herself, *the regular routine of a Sunday church service reminds her of happier times when her parents were still together.*

That morning Mara again declined breakfast, so while she was showering Del fixed herself something to eat. She had told the girl that they needed to leave a little earlier this day, because Father Mike was coming to St. Bernard's at 11:30 in case anyone wanted to go to confession before Mass. Mara didn't say much on the ride into town.

Del wondered what she could suggest to occupy the girl while she herself was at confession, but she need not have worried. When they saw the condition of the bouquets around the altar – "obviously brought this week by someone who doesn't know *beans* about which flowers last longer than a day," Del whispered to Mara – the teenager offered to take them into the maintenance room and freshen them up.

After Mass they didn't hang around long. Del asked someone else to lock up because the girl looked paler than usual, and she wanted to take her home and get some nourishment into her. It wasn't until after they had eaten lunch that the girl seemed to perk up, more like her old self.

"That was a long and tiring day yesterday, wasn't it?" asked Del, and the girl answered, "Yeah, but it was fun."

Pushing the dirty dishes aside, they sat and talked for awhile about the events of the day before. Then Mara, curious what "confession" was, asked Del about it.

"Well," Del began, "the meaning of confession starts with the understanding that we all commit sin. In your Sunday school, did you learn what 'sin' is?"

The girl nodded.

"Yeah, doing something wrong, like going against the Ten Commandments or something like that."

"Very true. And when we sin, we hurt God and we hurt ourselves and other people. But when we confess our sins to God and are truly sorry for them, he forgives us."

The girl looked puzzled.

"You have to go into that little room at a certain time to ask God to forgive your sins?"

Del smiled a little, unsure if she was explaining herself well.

"Not exactly," she said. "You can pray to God anytime you want and tell him you're sorry, and he forgives you if you're sincere. But in the Bible, in the book of James, it's clear that we are also supposed to confess our sins to another person."

In the manner so typical of Del, a big smile broke across her face as she exclaimed, "And I don't know about you, but I'm so grateful I don't have to go to Richard and confess my deepest, darkest sins to him!"

The look on the girl's face indicated that she was thinking what a disaster it would be to have to tell one's sins to Richard.

"So," Del continued, "Catholic priests hear our confessions when we go to them, and they can also give advice to help with any difficulties. There's a screen set up in that little room you saw, so the priest doesn't even have to know who I am unless I want him to know. And look here in the Bible..."

She trotted off to the living room and came back toting a Bible, riffling through its well-worn pages looking for a particular passage.

"See here, where it says that Jesus breathed on them – meaning the Apostles – and said to them, 'Receive the Holy Spirit; if you forgive the sins of any, they are forgiven; if you retain the sins of any, they are retained.' What do you think that means?"

Mara looked interested, but confused.

"I don't know," she admitted. "It sounds as if Jesus was giving them the power to forgive other people's sins. But what does 'retain' mean?"

"It means to keep things as they are, or, in other words, to *not* forgive them. So how would they know what to forgive, or not forgive, unless people confessed their sins to them?"

"But why wouldn't they forgive them?"

Del thought a minute.

"Well, it's true that any sin is forgivable, because God is merciful and he loves us so much. But I guess if a person would go to confession yet not be truly sorry for committing a sin, or even plan to go out and do it again, the priest could refuse that person absolution."

"What's absolution?"

"That's where the priest absolves, or forgives, the person of their sins, *'in the name* of the Father and of the Son and of the Holy Spirit.'"

Mara didn't say anything else but pushed back her chair, looking under the table to see if the kittens were awake. Realizing that Mama Cat was in the box nursing her babies, she helped Del clear the lunch dishes.

As Del filled the sink with dishwater, the girl suddenly said, "I don't think my church had anything like that. At least, I don't remember it."

"Did your church believe in the Bible?"

"Of course. They were always teaching from the Bible."

Del didn't say anything else right away while she washed the breakfast and lunch dishes and handed them to Mara to dry.

She seemed to be deep in thought, and after few quiet minutes had passed she asked, "Mara, did I tell you the story of how I met my husband?"

The girl shook her head.

"Well, I think I told you about how I ran away from home, my aunt's home, really, after my father died in that awful accident. And how I managed to get myself into lots of things that were pretty bad. I completely fell away from the Catholic faith I was raised in. I got hooked up with a group of people who seemed kind to me at first and gave me a place to crash, but they were heavy into parties and booze and drugs. There was stealing going on and just about every other thing you can imagine. People got hurt, *I* got hurt, and I hurt others." She stopped and sighed, but didn't elaborate on her last remark.

"Sometimes it wasn't easy waking up in the morning to face another day of craziness. But at the time it seemed that *anything* was better than the pain in my heart from my daddy's death. I just can't imagine where I would have ended up if Joey hadn't come into my life."

"Your husband?"

Del nodded.

"He started coming with a youth group from a local church – he was one of their adult leaders – and they'd stand on street corners talking to anyone who'd stop long enough to listen. They also handed out cookies and apples. I think that's why I first stopped. I was hungry! They were very nice and talked to me about how much Jesus loved me. And before I knew it I was going to their church with them. We studied the Bible together and I joined their church. Then, for some incomprehensible reason, Joe fell in love with me. I can't imagine what he saw in me 'cause I was a real mess! But he loved me more than I loved myself. It was through him that I finally came to really know how much God loved me. He was such a good man!"

It took a minute until Del, her hands deep in the dishwater, was able to go on. She blinked away tears as best she could and continued, "We got married and were very active in that church, me in the women's group – and before long the mom's club! – and Joey leading Bible studies for men. I was happy in that church and we had so many wonderful friends who loved the Lord with all their hearts.

"But I still carried around deep inside me all the wrong things I had done. Over and over I confessed them to God, but I had a hard time really believing that he forgave me. I had told Joe everything before we got married. I wanted him to know what he was getting into! He kept telling me to just 'leave it at the foot of the cross.' But it was so hard to do."

Del drained the sink, dried her hands and sat back down at the table, determined to finish her story. Mara sat down cross-legged on the floor and picked up the gold kitten that had jumped out of the box.

Del continued, "One day I was out walking with my little ones in a stroller and I happened to pass a Catholic church. All of a sudden I had an overwhelming desire to go to confession. So I hurried into that church before I could change my mind. I found a priest to hear my confession, and I can't imagine what that poor man must've thought!

"But I tell you, child," Del leaned down to where Mara was, "when I walked out of there, I finally felt as if I'd been set free! At last, God's forgiveness was real to me. By the grace of God I started going to Mass again, and then Joe started studying and reading about the Church and he eventually became Catholic too."

By this time Mara was quickly losing interest in the story, so Del left her playing with the kittens and went off to her favorite chair in the living room. She picked up her rosary and began to pray, remembering gratefully all the mercy and forgiveness that Jesus had poured into her wounded heart.

31

The Mystery Garden

The weeds were getting a little ahead of the flowers, so the next morning both of them were busy pulling out quack grass, ground ivy and the tenacious bindweed with its small white flowers so much like morning glories. While the woman worked her way systematically through the gardens on the left side of the backyard, Mara concentrated her efforts on the opposite side near a large tree at the far end.

It was a very attractive setting here in the filtered shade of the tree. A green metal bench invited anyone who was hot and weary to sit and enjoy the lovely garden for awhile. Every time Mara felt overwhelmed by the July sun, she'd break off her task of weeding and rest on the bench, taking sips from the bottle of water Del had left there for her. On one such break, she noticed the feathery plumes of creamy white and brilliant red flowers that seemed to thrive in the dappled light and went get the garden maps from the house.

Astilbe, she decided upon her return, matching the flowers with their location on the paper she held in her hand. *And those plants with the huge leaves must be the fragrant hostas.* She leaned down to sniff them. *Hmm, not too fragrant, really. Maybe they have to bloom to smell good.*

She identified the primroses, wild geraniums and Virginia bluebells by their leaves and position in the garden, as their spring blossoms were long spent. Plucking off a few dead flowers still clinging to them, she noticed that good portions of the shade were filled with the short pointed leaves of lily-of-the-valley.

Those I recognize, she thought to herself, then quickly turned her mind away from memories of the shaded garden encircling her own house – the only home she'd known until recently.

Take one day at a time. Concentrate on the job at hand.

She resolutely made her way to the next garden, a small semi-circular one beyond the tree in the back corner of the yard. Kneeling down and reaching to pull some weeds, she stopped with her hand in mid-air.

That's odd. I don't remember seeing rocks in the other gardens. In fact, Del showed me her rock garden. The girl glanced over to where the woman was working. *She said her husband had dug up every single rock from the backyard and put them over there where she planted flowers between them.*

Mara leaned forward a bit so that she could push aside the plants that partially covered the two melon-size rocks. She was surprised to see both rocks had flowers painted on their fronts. Beneath each picture there was a day and a year brushed on in black. The dates were nearly thirty years ago, and this one was, what? She pondered a moment. *About a year after that one?*

She recognized one of the painted flowers. *A rose!* Then she realized that the low bush which shaded the rock had ivory-colored roses blooming on it. She sat back on her heels, deep in thought. It had suddenly occurred to her that, of all the multitudes of beautiful plants here in Windmill Gardens, she had never seen any other roses.

Isn't that kind of odd? You'd think a garden this size would have lots of roses. Everyone who loves flowers loves roses.

She didn't recognize the flower on the other rock, which, like the rose, was the same as on the plant overshadowing it. She went to the bench to get the garden maps, and then was able to identify the "Veronica" with its spikes of pinkish-red blossoms. Next she turned her attention to the other flowers in the garden, first of all the tall sky-blue ones along the back.

Delphiniums! So that's what delphiniums look like. They're beautiful – no wonder Del was fascinated with them when she was little. The rest of the garden was filled with purple catmint, mounds of chrysanthemums which had yet to bloom, and delicate baby's breath which nestled like a fine white mist between the others.

Still puzzled, Mara settled down to weed the mystery garden. *I'll ask Del later,* she thought. But by the time she had finished with that garden and had moved on to the adjoining one, the noontime sun was making her feel quite light-headed. She was grateful when the woman called her in for lunch, and completely forgot about her question until much later.

That afternoon in the woods, not far from the stream they had visited before, Del discovered to her delight that the wild black raspberries were ripe.

"The red raspberries in my garden won't be ready for at least another week. We'll make these black ones into a streusel-topped cobbler to take to the picnic tomorrow. Just see if Richard makes a fuss about eating wild foods!"

She had thought ahead to bring along plastic bowls with lids so the berries wouldn't get crushed, and they filled a half-dozen of these and stowed them in Del's backpack. They picked nothing else that afternoon as Del wanted to have time to make the dessert. But she pointed out the elderberry bushes growing densely along the edges of the creek. Their distinctive flowers, umbrella-like clusters of delicate white, were just beginning to open.

"The tiny berries that'll set in August don't taste very good fresh. But they cook up into a wonderful syrup that's good for the immune system. Elderberry syrup costs a fortune in the store!"

I think I've heard all this before, went through the girl's mind as they re-entered the woods. Mara had become very familiar with this area, so she was able to lead the way along the crisscrossing paths back into the meadow behind Windmill Gardens. She noticed that the white clover which had previously brightened this clearing was now overshadowed by the taller purple red clover. After they paused to admire a butterfly perched on a blossom, she and the woman continued into the backyard. That's when she remembered to ask Del about the painted rocks.

The woman stopped to look where Mara was pointing. She was silent for a moment. At last, the only thing she said, almost to herself, was, "Child, those rocks are my reminder of God's mercy to me."

Del wiped her forehead with the back of her hand, glanced at the girl who didn't understand what she was talking about and suggested they go in out of the hot sun and bake that cobbler.

32

Fourth of July

On the way to the Spencer farm the next afternoon, the two of them were betting whether or not they thought Richard would try the salad Del was bringing. Del believed that, while Richard always spouted off about her "weeds," he'd have the gumption to at least try the new dish. Mara insisted, "No way!" Their discussion was short by necessity, since their destination was just down the road.

Richard and Sean greeted them and it didn't take long for Abby to come running and grab onto Mara's hand. Richard introduced them to his parents and younger brothers, and Ann stuck her head out the farmhouse door, calling for Del to bring her food to the kitchen. The smell of grilling hot dogs and hamburgers was in the air, and the picnic area, otherwise known as the front lawn, was suitably decorated for the occasion with small American flags around the perimeter. Abby dragged Mara around to show off the construction-paper chains with red, white and blue links dangling awkwardly from tree branches.

Ann's call, "Time to eat!" was met by cheers from all the hungry folks at the picnic. The young people scrambled into the house first, followed more slowly by the adults, to load their plates at the smorgasbord laid out on the kitchen table. Then they returned outside to choose a meat from the grill ably tended by Richard. He cheerfully wore one of his wife's flowered aprons, his face flushed from the heat but never losing its broad smile.

He asked Del what kind of food she had brought over, but she just informed him with an impish grin he'd have to find out on his own. As soon as everyone was served, he went into the house and returned with a piled-up plate. It seemed as if he had taken a little of everything. Del looked over at Mara and winked, while Richard kept up a constant banter with one and all as he ate. Del and the girl surreptitiously watched him work his way around the plate towards the salad which, actually, didn't *look* much different from a regular green salad – if you didn't count the flecks of orange from chopped daylilies. Mara was eating it willingly, having discovered that she liked her lettuce mixed with wild greens. Seeing a forkful of it go into Richard's mouth, she glanced over at Del and mouthed, "You win!"

Del said nothing until Richard had finished his entire plate, and then she asked him how he had enjoyed her salad. The good-natured man just chuckled and said everything was delicious, and that he really didn't *want* to know which dish had weeds in it. The black raspberry cobbler went over well with young and old alike. Del felt she had to point out that the berries could be considered "weeds," since they grew in the woods.

Richard's father, who had met his son's unusual neighbor on other occasions, asked her point-blank why she gathered food in the wild when she could buy anything she needed at a grocery store. Del countered with a question of her own.

"Bill, why do you and your sons like to go fishing when you can just go to the store and buy fish?"

They all laughed and agreed that, indeed, Del had a point there.

The meal ended with the making of homemade ice cream. Richard brought out his grandparents' old-fashioned ice cream maker and had the children use wooden mallets to hammer a cloth sack filled with ice cubes. When there was enough crushed ice, he layered it alternately with rock salt around the metal canister in the center. Then Ann brought out the chilled cream-and-sugar mixture. She poured it into the canister and her husband screwed on the lid with the attached paddle.

The children clamored to take turns turning the handle, and Richard added more ice and salt as needed. As the cream thickened and got harder to mix, the adults helped with some of the labor. Soon Abby was allowed to lick off the wooden paddle while Richard spooned out the icy smooth, creamy dessert for everyone.

The entertainment that day consisted of Abby twirling a large plastic hoop around her tiny waist. She insisted that everyone else try it too. Mara adamantly refused and Ann begged off, patting her swollen stomach and claiming she wouldn't fit inside the hoop. Richard's brother gave it a few hopeless whirls until it dropped to the ground. However, Del surprised the picnickers by keeping the hoop going around and around her ample middle for the longest time, and they all applauded her feat.

Abby tried to get Mara to go see the kittens, but the girl shook her head, brushing off the child. After a time, Abby and Sean went to play by themselves while the adults settled back in their lawn chairs to catch up on local news.

Richard said, "Guess what, Del! You know what I saw yesterday at Wally's?"

Ann leaned a little closer to Mara and clued her in. "That's Wally's Feed Store," she explained.

Del's face fell and she exclaimed, "Don't tell me!"

Richard nodded. "Yep. Right there in the front window was the juiciest, ripest tomato you've ever seen!"

This time it was Richard's mom on the other side of Mara who turned to her and asked, "Did they tell you about the tomato contest we have hereabouts every year?"

Mara nodded, watching Del's crestfallen face.

The older woman continued, "Well, Wally always displays in his store window the first ripe tomato of the season. He even prints up a little sign with the grower's name on it. Del's had the honor many times over the years, but it looks this year like someone's beat her to it!"

Del, frowning, asked Richard, "Okay, tell me who it is!"

Richard's face broke into a broad smile, and he watched Del's face closely as he replied, "Well…it's Henry."

"Henry! It's *Henry?*" Del seemed scandalized. "Why that…!" She stopped herself and took a deep breath. Then she huffed, "Now how does Wally know that Henry didn't cheat again, like he did six years ago?!"

Ann broke in to explain to Mara how Henry Stedmann had taken one of the tomatoes his sister Martha had brought with her when she drove up to visit from the South, and tried to pass it off as his own home-grown.

"It was his own sister who told on him, and then he claimed it was just a joke! Can you believe it?" Del spouted off. Mara, for her part, seemed incredulous that something as silly as this tomato contest could be taken so seriously.

Richard threw up his hands, shrugged his broad shoulders and grinned. "All I know is that Wally claimed he saw the tomato with his own eyes, growin' in Henry's garden. Del, you'll have to take it up with Wally."

Del's eyes narrowed, but her sense of humor had returned. "I just wonder if Wally checked closely to make sure it wasn't spray-painted!"

There were chuckles all around at Del's remark, then the conversation turned to other topics. It wasn't long before she was relating stories about her growing-up years.

"Del, tell us about the geese," Richard egged her on, having heard the tale before.

"You mean the ones we had on the farm? Gosh, those crazy birds were better than a watch dog! When anyone would pull into the driveway, the geese would set up such a racket, honking and flapping their wings. Let me tell you, it was loud enough to wake the dead!

"And the old gander was the worst. You couldn't go anywhere near him or he'd attack. He'd hold his long neck down in front of him like a battering ram and run at you. And he sure could bite! So when he'd take a run at me, I'd throw him."

"What do you mean, 'throw him?'" asked Richard's mother.

"Just what I said. I'd grab him by his neck behind his head, and throw him as far as I could. Then the rest of the geese would go off after him, flapping and honking." They all thought the image of Del throwing geese was pretty hilarious.

"Wouldn't he come back?"

"Oh, he never learned. The very next time he'd do it again, and I'd throw him again. Geese must be stupid – or very persistent!" Del shook her head, grinning.

Richard's parents had brought sparklers for the kids. The children waved them around through the air, enjoying them even though it was still daylight. While everyone else was thus engaged, Del and Ann went in to clean up the kitchen.

"Del," asked Ann, covering up the last of the food and putting it away, "what's wrong with Mara? She seems even quieter than usual, like she's depressed."

"I know. She's also more tired than someone of her age should be, and sometimes doesn't even want to eat. But then again, who wouldn't be depressed in her situation?"

"Has she said anything about why she left home?"

"Well, I've tried to bring up the subject, but she seemed to be frightened. So I haven't pushed it. All I know is, she believes her mother doesn't care about her."

"Does she have any other relatives?"

"Yes, her father, but he walked out on them about four years ago. She has a letter he wrote to her, and that was her last contact with him."

Del took the wet dish that Ann had just washed and began to dry it with a linen towel. She continued, "I get the impression from the little she's told me that she left home in a hurry. Didn't take much with her and didn't know where she was going. She had her dad's letter in her purse, but only thought about trying to find him after she'd been on her own a day or so. Actually, we *did* try to phone him not too long ago."

"What happened?"

"Not much. The number she had for him was disconnected. I tried calling information, but there was no one by that name anywhere in that area. Mara was crushed, but I assured her that it was no problem if she continued to stay with me and help in the garden."

"But what about school in the fall?"

Del sighed. "I don't know. Also, even if she doesn't think so, there's someone, somewhere, who's worried sick about her."

Ann drained the dishwater and dried her hands. "Don't you think you should notify the authorities?"

"I'm afraid she'll take off again. And I certainly don't want to see her returned into what may be an abusive situation. Maybe I'm wrong, but I think she's best off staying with me for the present."

Del wiped the table and hung the dishcloth over the sink, then stood there a moment looking out the window toward the barn, deep in thought.

"Every time I pray about it, which is all the time, I just keep getting the impression that I need to wait for God's leading," she said reflectively.

"Well, how do you know you're hearing him right?" Ann asked.

Del shook her head. "I don't know for certain. But I believe that when we try with all our hearts to put God first in everything, he guides us and gives us what we need in every situation.

"So," she said, turning to Ann and giving her a hug, "thanks for inviting us today, and please pray that everything will turn out for the best for Mara."

33

Garden Tours

The next few weeks were busy as usual. Del had Mara work at tidying up the garden by dead-heading spent blooms and pulling any stray weeds that popped up here and there. She also charged her with keeping an eye on the rapidly-growing peaches, picking up fallen ones and watching for insect invasions, even though peaches were one of the easier fruits she grew.

"I guess the bugs don't like the feel of the fuzz," Del remarked, stroking the velvet skin of one of the peaches. "You'll notice that I don't have any apple trees. I tried growing them years ago. But it was so hard to keep insects from infesting the apples without using poisonous sprays that I finally gave up."

Other fruit was ripening, and they picked red raspberries and the large pie cherries. What they couldn't eat right away, they put in the freezer. Del explained that in the cooler weather she'd use the frozen fruit to make her famous jellies and jams to sell at the farmer's market.

Out in the woods they found mulberries, blackberries, gooseberries and serviceberries free for the taking. The woman also pointed out the clusters of green buckthorn berries on their ubiquitous glossy-leaved bushes, warning her of their poisonous properties even after they turned an attractive deep-purple in fall.

In the vegetable plot, Del's tomatoes were turning bright red, and they enjoyed fresh sliced tomatoes on their salads and sandwiches. Any surplus of these, too, was frozen, to be made into tomato sauce in cooler weather. Digging under the mulch in the patch where potato vines ran rampant, they would pull out early potatoes and served them baked with farm-fresh butter and chopped chives from the garden. Other vegetables were also starting to produce and the eating was mighty fine at this point in the summer.

This was also the season for tours of Windmill Gardens. Garden clubs would phone Del and arrange to bring out a group for the purpose of touring her fabulous backyard. Del never turned them down, even though it was certainly an inconvenience at this busy time. A bus would come roaring down the road in a cloud of dust, park across from the giant mailbox and disgorge a whole slew of people. These were mostly ladies, although occasionally a white-haired gentleman or two came with them. Del would open wide the gates on the far side of the house and, with a broad smile, welcome them all to her garden.

She even went so far as to have a plate of cookies and a pitcher of lemonade waiting for them at the table on the patio. Mara generally stayed in the house during these tours, resentful of the influx of strangers into the peaceful atmosphere of what she was coming to think of as *her* garden. Del noticed her attitude and gently reminded the girl that the flowers were God's gifts, and it was a joy to share them with others. She didn't insist that the girl come outside during these tours, but Mara often found herself involved anyway as one person or another would knock on the back door requesting to use the bathroom.

Once in awhile, children came with their parents. Mara would watch, upset, through the kitchen window as they would run unsupervised down the garden paths and even pick flowers without permission. But Del always laughed off the parents' embarrassed apologies, hugging the little ones and saying that children were more important than plants.

Del truly enjoyed people, and it was evident in the caring manner in which she led them through the gardens and patiently answered their questions – no matter how repetitive some of them were. She never seemed to get tired of singling out special plants or identifying flowers. Mara began to wonder why Del didn't have copies made of her garden maps to hand out to visitors. She decided to broach the subject one evening at supper, and the woman was surprised and pleased.

"Why, child, what a good idea! I never thought of it! It would help people to know which plant is which. Let's do that the next time we go into town."

Del accepted Mara's generous offer to re-draw the maps in ink so that they would copy clearly, and the girl spent many hours engaged in this endeavor. She also played with the kittens more as they got bigger, watching them pounce on each other and chase after a string pulled along the floor. She loved them all, but her favorite was Ginger. The gold kitten would climb partway up the girl's blue-jeaned leg with her tiny sharp claws, then she'd realize the hopelessness of trying to get down again and would mew pitifully. The girl would laugh, pluck her off and nestle her fuzzy warmth next to her cheek.

Del always enjoyed watching the girl and kitten playing together, because it was then that Mara forgot about her problems for a while and seemed more relaxed and happier. The woman never gave up praying for her, not only during her quiet time set aside with the Lord but also as she worked. She still didn't understand exactly what God wanted her to do. Oh, she certainly told him many times that she'd be happy to help him out if he needed it. But he didn't seem to be taking her up on the offer.

Day after day went by, set to the quiet rhythm of the ongoing work in the tranquil garden. It was well into the third week of July, with Del thinking maybe she should come up with *something* to get the situation with the girl off dead center, when it was Mara herself who made a surprising statement.

34

Connected Again

Del was drying the last of the lunch dishes while an electric fan on a nearby counter stirred the hot, muggy air. She wiped the back of her arm across her damp forehead and smiled at Mara, seated cross-legged on the floor with three fuzzy kittens clambering over her legs.

"They sure are cute, aren't they?" Del asked, breaking the silence which had descended since their meal finished. The girl didn't respond. She seemed to have something on her mind so, without another word, Del simply hung the sodden dish towel on its rack and started to walk into the living room.

Suddenly the girl glanced up at her, saying, "I wish I could let my friend Peter know that I'm all right."

Del stopped, looked at the girl, then went over to one of the kitchen chairs and dropped heavily into it. She kept silent, waiting for Mara to go on.

"I mean, he must be awfully worried by now."

No kidding, thought Del. *Not to mention her family. But this is encouraging – she's finally thinking about someone else.*

"Well," said Del, "what do you think you should do?"

The girl bit her lip and shook her head. "I don't know. I was thinking of calling him. But what if his mother answers the phone? His mom and mine have been neighbors forever. She'd be sure to tell my mother."

A shadow flickered across Mara's face and Del could see fear in her eyes. *Whatever has happened to this child,* wondered Del, *that she's so afraid to have contact with her own mother?*

"Why don't you write him a letter?"

Mara shook her head again. "I thought of that. But his parents would probably be the ones to pick up the mail."

Del sat thinking silently. She didn't want to say the wrong thing since this was finally a breakthrough with the girl. All of a sudden her face lit up and she shared her thought with Mara.

"What if," she said, her eyes dancing, "you e-mail him?"

The girl's mouth literally dropped open and the surprise on her face was almost comical.

"E-mail him! *E-mail?* You have a *computer?*"

"Of course I have a computer! Doesn't everyone have a computer nowadays?"

Del chuckled at the look on the girl's face, thinking to herself, *Well, it's true that I have one, but do I tell her that I can't figure out how to use it?*

Del beckoned to her, saying, "Come on," and Mara carefully placed the kittens back into their box. Del unplugged the fan to take it with her and opened the door into her son's old bedroom. She flicked on the overhead light and set the fan rotating on the floor before putting up the shades to let in some daylight.

Mara looked over at the desk against the far wall, and what to her wondering eyes should appear but a *computer.* It was covered up with a sheet of dusty plastic but was definitely a computer nonetheless. She just stared at it dumbly while Del pulled off the covering, apologizing as she did so.

"It's not the most up-to-date model, I'm afraid. After my son bought himself a fancy new one last year, he brought his old one home and set it up for me. He hooked it up to the internet and everything. Said he wanted me to stay in touch with him by e-mail. But," Del winced at admitting her abysmal ignorance, "after he left I totally forgot what he taught me, and I haven't been able to figure it out since."

I'm really awful at this kind of thing! Even having him tell me over the phone how to do it hasn't helped. But he did promise to write it all down for me – when he's not so busy!

Inviting the incredulous girl to sit down, she drew up another chair and sat next to Mara, asking, "So, do *you* know how to use this thing?" *That's a dumb question, Del! Kids today cut their teeth on computers.*

They both searched a moment for the ON switch, then Mara pushed the monitor button and the screen lit up in front of them. The girl didn't seem to have any trouble knowing what to do next, and Del watched fascinated as Mara found her way through this program and that. She finally turned to Del and asked if she'd like to learn how to access her e-mail account.

"Not right now," Del answered, stating that the hot weather was making her feel extremely sleepy and that she wanted to rest awhile and say her prayers. She told Mara there were some games on the computer that she was welcome to use.

Del went to the living room and dozed for quite some time in her easy chair. When she awoke it was nearly suppertime, but she had made no plans to go out wilding in the heat that day anyway. She could see the girl still at the computer in the bedroom, the light from the screen playing across her face, so she went to the kitchen and began putting together a simple cold supper.

Mara finally shut everything down and came to the table to eat. She looked distracted and more tired than usual, so Del waited until she got some food into her to ask how things were going with the computer.

"Good," Mara answered noncommittally. "It was fun playing some games after all this time."

The girl kept her head down while eating, and it wasn't until she was nearly finished that she looked over at Del and said quietly, "Pete was awfully glad to hear from me. He said he couldn't believe it was really me." She pushed her lanky hair back from her face and Del could see the girl's troubled expression.

"Anything else?" she asked quietly.

Mara seemed reluctant to continue, but she finally did.

"He said that my mother had called the police after I left home and they searched everywhere, but no one had seen me."

Uh, oh. I wonder if I can get in trouble for harboring a runaway. But Del didn't let on about her own misgivings. She just listened.

"Pete was afraid something awful had happened to me. But I just said I was staying with a nice lady."

Del smiled, then asked, "Did you mention where I live?"

The girl shook her head.

"No, and I told him not to tell his mom or mine that he'd heard from me."

Sighing, Mara got up to take her dirty dishes to the sink. Del, figuring that the conversation had been brought to an end, merely suggested that they needed to do some work in the cooler garden before darkness set in that evening.

35

Another Mother

In the mornings following, life went on as before at Windmill Gardens. The two of them weeded, watered and did all the things that were necessary to keep a garden of this size looking and producing its best. There were also flowers to be cut and dried for Del's winter projects. It was important to harvest them precisely at the right time, just as they were beginning to bloom. If one waited until the flowers were entirely open, the petals might fall off as they dried.

Del showed the girl how to cut yarrow, liatris, baby's breath and the blue-stemmed sea holly, strip off their leaves and bundle them tightly with rubber bands. Then they would hang the bunches upside-down from clothesline in the garage where a fan gently circulated the air. Long stems of larkspur and bee balm were added, along with a selection of herbs.

When the heat in the afternoon wasn't too unbearable, they also gathered a lot of cattails and prickly teasels from the woods, along with the tall flower stalks of mullein with its soft velvety leaves. Almost everything Del picked was amenable to being air-dried, although she sand- or silica-dried a few flowers, like astilbe, so their colors wouldn't fade. Mara was a quick learner. With her help Del was able to gather and dry more material than in previous years.

Yet, although the girl still pitched in willingly to help with the gardening chores, there was a subtle shift in her focus with the introduction of the computer. Now it often seemed as if most work was done with the intention of getting through as quickly as possible in order to have more time on the computer. Gone was any interest she had previously shown in learning about the wild, and more than once Del found herself getting a little irritated at having to compete for the girl's attention.

However, there was a positive side to all this. Mara offered to show Del step-by-step how to e-mail her son in Germany. Once she became adept at it, Del was thrilled to be able to keep in touch with him so easily – and cheaply! She also obtained her son Robert's address and soon e-mails were flying back and forth between his family and Del.

One day Mara asked the woman, "Since you like to mail-order things, why don't you do it online?"

Online? You can buy stuff online? Del, still a computer neophyte, was astonished and intrigued. She fetched one of her favorite gardening catalogs, picked out a few items she had been meaning to buy and the girl showed her how to use her credit card to order.

This is terrific, thought Del. *And way too easy! If I'm not careful I'll run over my credit limit.*

Mara was happy to be able to help out Del this way, and overall seemed to be in a better mood from being in contact with Peter. She shared with Del some of the events going on in her hometown, or what Pete said this friend or that was doing. Even though she was careful not to mention anything about her own family, Del always listened with great interest.

One morning they were out in the garden, watching the butterflies and bees busy about their work in the flowers. Del called the girl's attention to some of the plants that were especially attractive to the graceful butterflies.

"You'll notice that they seem to like purple flowers the best. Like that Russian sage," she stated, gesturing to a plant whose froth of tiny blossoms resembled a light-purple mist. "Over there are heliotrope, Joe Pye weed – that's a native American plant – and coneflowers, those tall ones that look a bit like daisies. Of course, the butterfly bush and butterfly weed attract lots of them. Those swallowtails you see over there especially go for the dillweed. One year I wanted to make pickles. But there was hardly any dill left to use because the swallowtail caterpillars ate it all!"

"There's some butterflies that aren't on purple flowers," Mara pointed out to Del.

The woman explained that they also liked the bright gold of coreopsis and marigolds, especially if they were mixed in with purple-hued flowers. "And further," she went on, "they seem to enjoy flat-topped flowers like daisies. Maybe they're like little landing pads for them!"

They were wending their way around the garden paths near the far left corner of the house. Here Del grew a beautiful deep-red clematis vine, which climbed on a trellis arched over a statue of the Blessed Mother. Although the girl had seen the statue before, this was the first time she mentioned it.

"Is that Mary?" she asked, and Del nodded.

"Why do you have a statue of her? Do you worship her?"

Mara, of course, didn't know that the idea of worshiping anyone other than God was abhorrent to faithful Del. But the woman realized the question had been asked in all innocence.

She gently responded, "No, child, the Blessed Virgin Mary isn't to be worshiped since she isn't God, but a human like you and me. Just as I have pictures of my family on my bedroom wall because I love them, I also have a crucifix in my living room because I love Jesus and this statue here because I love Mary. Don't you carry a picture of your little sister in your wallet because you love her? All these things, these images, are visual reminders of those we care about."

Del picked a few spent flowers off the vine, then continued, "Since I love Jesus, it's natural for me to love his mother too. You know, a long time ago when my own mother died – and me still a teenager! – I felt so lonely. One day I just up and told Jesus that I needed a mother! And it was so strange. That very day I picked up my Bible and it opened at the place where Jesus was on the cross saying, 'Behold your mother!' And I believe with all my heart that my Mother Mary was praying for me during those years I turned away from God."

"What do you mean, praying for you? She's dead, isn't she?" At Mara's quizzical look Del smiled.

"Child, anyone who lived and died in God's friendship, and is with him in heaven, isn't really dead. He or she is more alive than we are!"

Mara had to think about that for awhile, and she had plenty of opportunity as they finished their chores and went in the house for lunch. Del removed the soiled linen runner in the center of the table and laid down a fresh one, and had Mara take down a heavy ceramic bowl from the cupboard to fill with fresh fruit for their meal.

"Watch out!" she warned. "Coco and Ginger are right next to your feet!"

These days, they had to be careful where they walked in the kitchen as the mischievous kittens were almost always underfoot. The girl cautiously stepped around the kittens and carried the bowl to the table. While they were eating, Mara returned to their previous conversation.

"How is it that a person can be friends with God? Isn't that kind of strange? I mean, he's *God,* and we're just...just... well, we're just *us!"*

So she does believe in God? We're making progress!

Del allowed as to how that was true, that we are just humans and God seems so far above us.

"But don't forget – Jesus is truly God, yet he received a human body from his mother Mary. So he is certainly like us. Knowing that, doesn't it make it a little easier to talk to him?"

Mara thought about that for a minute.

"Talk to him?" she finally asked. "Aren't you supposed to *pray* to Jesus?"

"Same difference," answered Del with a smile. "Now tell me, what do you think is the reason that one person talks to another? Say, you see a new girl at school and you think you'd like to be friends with her. What would be the purpose behind you starting up a conversation with her?"

"Well, I guess to get to know her better – what she's like, what she enjoys doing, stuff like that."

Del nodded. "Right. Can you imagine trying to be friends with someone and never talking to them? Well, if we want to get to know Jesus, we have to start up a conversation with him. Call it praying if you want. I myself talk to him all day long. He's the only person who never gets tired of listening to me!"

"But how do you carry on a conversation with someone who doesn't talk to *you*?"

At that insightful question, Del thought of her own prayers which seemed so one-sided lately as she begged God to give her some answers.

But, she sighed to herself, *I know that sometimes God seems silent so that we can learn to trust him. I guess, Lord, that you're teaching me even as I attempt to teach this child.*

Del responded, with certitude in her voice, "He will, child, he will. He hears all our prayers, and sometimes we can hear his voice in our hearts. More often, though, he speaks to us through Scripture – like what I told you earlier about him sharing his own mother with me – and he speaks through his Church, and he speaks through other people and the everyday things of our lives. But to understand what he's saying to us, we have to be persistent in prayer and not give up, even when it's hard to keep praying."

Mara was quiet for awhile, watching the kittens playing at her feet. At last she looked up at Del with a question.

"What do you do if you don't know how to pray?"

Del smiled widely, answering, "Just talk to him like you're talking to me! Tell him you don't know how to begin, but that you'd like to get to know him better. Ask him to teach you about himself, and don't stop asking. I can guarantee, this is one prayer that God is most happy to answer!"

36

End of July

Del had a shiny metal colander upside-down on her head, its little feet sticking up like primitive horns. "Viking queen" was the thought that popped into Mara's mind when she first saw the woman sitting on the bench under the shade tree in the backyard. Del was entertaining Sean and Abby with fantastic adventure tales of knights and kings and fair maidens needing to be rescued. Sean was listening closely and trying not to laugh too often or too loudly. But Del *was* absolutely comical and even Mara was having a hard time suppressing a grin.

Little Abby had no such inhibitions, shrieking with delight and jumping up frequently to clap her hands. Every so often the storyteller would pause, peer out at the children from under her strikingly unusual helmet, and in a deep, melodramatic voice ask them, "And *what* do you think happened *next*?"

Then her story would spontaneously take off in a new direction, depending on what the youngsters came up with. Mara listened with one ear while weeding a nearby garden. Here, the hollyhocks with their old-fashioned pink flowers towered over the black-eyed Susans and mounds of thick-leaved sedum which were yet to bloom. This was the last garden which needed to be tidied up for the garden club tour coming the next afternoon.

It was earlier that morning that Ann had called to ask Del to watch the children for her while she visited the doctor for her monthly check-up. Apparently, Richard was not home and her mother-in-law was ill and couldn't do it, so kind-hearted Del said she wouldn't mind and would send Mara down to fetch them. The girl was somewhat surprised at that last statement. The woman knew she had a license, but that she hadn't driven for several months. Del seemed certain, though, that the girl couldn't go far wrong just driving down the country road a little ways and back again.

She watched as the girl carefully backed the old green boat down the driveway, and stood by the mailbox until her car was safely on its way back home again with Mara and the children. Now they were all out in the garden on this beautiful morning in late July, waiting for Ann to return.

Story time over, Sean went to help Del move some flower pots to a different location, while his little sister hopped, skipped and jumped her way over to see what Mara was doing. Squatting down next to the teenage girl who was weeding and spreading straw for a mulch, Abby asked the age-old question of children everywhere.

"Whatcha doin'?"

So Mara patiently pointed out the difference between the flowers and weeds, even while reflecting that, in Del's way of looking at things, the weeds had just as much value as the garden plants. But she didn't try to explain it all to the child, who had quickly lost interest anyway. Now Abby was expounding on her excitement of going back to school soon and seeing her friends. At that, Mara got a little irritable. She changed the subject and was much relieved when Ann finally returned.

"Mommy!" yelled Abby, spying her mother coming down the garden path with Del.

"Hi, sweetie. Did you miss me?"

Ann gave her daughter a hug and Abby ran off to see what Sean was doing on the patio.

"How was your check-up?" asked Del, and the younger woman, looking extremely tired, shook her head.

"The baby has dropped down into position already, and I still have six weeks to go," she grimaced, rubbing the side of her big stomach. "The doctor wants me to stay off my feet. Can you imagine?" Ann chuckled glumly.

"You have to stay in bed?" Del asked, her eyebrows arched as if she couldn't think how Ann would be able to manage such a thing.

"Well, no, I can get up and do things, but every chance I get I'm supposed to lie down. I guess I'll have to depend on the kids to help out more."

As Ann got ready to leave with the children, Del assured her that she and Mara would do what they could. And Del was as good as her word, sending Mara down often with casseroles and baked goods. Several times a week they would both go and help

Ann with the laundry and housecleaning. They didn't see much of Richard, since when he wasn't doing work on his own farm, he was over helping his family with theirs. Sean took on more responsibility with the chickens. And Abby? Well, Abby tried to help out her mommy but usually ended up causing such a big mess that it was hardly worth it.

With everything going on, there was less time for Mara to spend on the computer or for Del to gather wildflowers for drying. They managed to get out in the woods only one more time in late July, and the girl was a surprised to see how the familiar meadows and fields had changed. The blue chicory in most of the open spaces was crowded out by the feathery-looking violet flowers of spotted knapweed, and the beautiful but invasive purple loosestrife had taken over everywhere there was a bit of dampness.

"What are those?" asked Mara, as they came across a large field covered by narrow-leaved plants with slender drooping panicles of white flowers.

Del answered, "Those are narrow-leaved plants with slender drooping panicles of white flowers." At the girl's surprised look, she laughed, shrugged her shoulders and exclaimed, "Well, I don't know *everything!*"

The end of the month was upon them almost before they realized it, and August made its hot and humid entrance on a sun-drenched Sunday morning with more of the girl's questions for Del.

37

Communion

Del had tried to talk the girl into having a little breakfast, but Mara declined and was just now emerging from the shower. The woman cleaned up her dishes and they both settled into kitchen chairs to enjoy the kittens playing on the floor. Mama Cat lay off to one side, her tail up in the air like a flag, its end twitching back and forth as she watched her babies' antics.

Ginger, always a little more adventuresome than the others, clawed herself up onto Mara's shoe and was playing with the laces. The girl smiled and reached down for the kitten, cuddling her on her lap and stroking the soft golden-orange fuzz that shaded into darker stripes across the back and head.

Del looked at Mara with concern. The girl still seemed so drawn and pale, although in the last six weeks she had put on enough weight that she hardly needed the belt any more to keep up her pants. Dark circles still shadowed her eyes, causing Del to wonder if she was sleeping well at night. She asked, but the girl just nodded without comment. Then the woman mentioned there were about fifteen minutes before they needed to leave for church, and that triggered a query from Mara.

"Why can't I receive Communion too?" she asked, dangling a string over the kitten's head and smiling at Ginger's clumsy attempts to snag it with a paw.

Del was surprised at the question, as the girl had continued to attend Mass with her every Sunday but had never broached the subject before. She had to think for a minute, taking off her glasses and rubbing her eyes before answering.

"Well," she replied, "I guess if you go to Communion at a Catholic Mass you are really declaring that you are 'in union,' so to speak, with millions of Catholics around the world and what we believe about the Eucharist."

At the word "Eucharist," Mara looked up at Del and said, "Oh, yeah. I saw that word on the wall behind the altar. What does it mean?"

Del considered for a moment whether she should explain that the word itself came from the Greek word meaning "to give thanks." But she decided that that was not what the girl was asking.

"The Holy Eucharist," began Del, "is the body and blood of Jesus Christ, under the appearances of bread and wine." But by the confused expression on Mara's face, she decided she had better simplify things, so she started again.

"Do you remember this story in the Bible? At the Last Supper, the night before he died on the cross, Jesus took some bread and wine, held them up and said, 'This is my body' and then, 'This is my blood.'"

Mara nodded, and Del continued.

"Well, Catholics believe that Jesus was speaking literally when he said that. The bread and wine actually became his flesh and blood. And when Father Mike says those very same words at Mass today, the bread and wine will become the very same body and blood of Jesus."

Mara looked shocked at Del's words, exclaiming, "You can't be serious!"

"But I am, child! Jesus never lied, and his words are meant for all time. He said, 'Do this in memory of me.'"

The girl rubbed her forehead, thinking.

"But surely, Jesus was just speaking symbolically. He didn't actually mean his *real* flesh and blood!"

Del went to get her Bible and thumbed through it until she found what she was looking for.

"Mara, look here in the sixth chapter of the gospel of John. First, Jesus says that *he* is the bread from heaven and that whoever eats this bread will live forever. Then he says that the bread he will give is *his flesh* for the life of the world."

She ran her finger down to the next paragraph.

"See, it says here that the Jews were quarreling among themselves, asking, 'How can this man give us his flesh to eat?' But Jesus didn't say, 'Don't worry, I'm only speaking symbolically.'

"You know, Mara, Jesus had called himself many things before, like a 'gate' or a 'vine,' and his followers hadn't been bothered by those statements. They never seemed to think he meant he was an *actual* gate or vine. But now, instead of correcting their ideas, he actually goes on to reinforce what he just said."

Del pointed to more verses in the same chapter of John.

"'Unless you eat the flesh of the Son of Man and drink his blood, you do not have life within you.' *And*, 'Whoever eats my flesh and drinks my blood has eternal life.' He even says, 'For my flesh is food indeed and my blood is drink indeed.' I'm not sure you could get any more clear than that."

Del stopped to clean her glasses on the bottom edge of her shirt. Mara shook her head, saying, "I still don't get it."

The woman, putting her glasses back on, indicated the following paragraphs where many of Jesus' disciples didn't get it, either.

"It says here that they went back to their former way of life and no longer went about with him. Yet he doesn't call them back and tell them that they misunderstood him."

Mara was unconvinced.

"Am I supposed to believe that Jesus is really present in that bread and wine? It seems pretty ordinary to me."

Del chuckled.

"I know, child. But don't forget that God was able to become a human baby – that is, Jesus. So he's certainly able to change these ordinary things into his own body and blood if he chooses to, even if it still looks and tastes like bread and wine to us. It takes faith to believe, and faith is a gift from God to those who want to receive it. Hey, now we have to get moving!"

Del stood up, grabbed her purse from the counter and the keys off a hook by the back door, and they hurried out to the garage. They began their drive in silence, but soon Mara asked, "So, if I believe that the bread and wine at Mass are the body and blood of Jesus, can I receive Communion too?"

The woman glanced over at her before replying.

"If someday you come to believe that it's really true, that Jesus is really present in the Eucharist, then you should become Catholic. That would be a public witness that you believe what Catholics believe. *But*," she continued, "you'd need to give it some time and a lot of prayer. It's not something to rush into."

Mara was quiet for most of the ride, but when they were nearing town she asked Del one more question.

"So, if what you told me is true, I wonder *why* would Jesus do such a thing? I mean, give us his body and blood as food and drink? It seems a little crazy, if you stop and think about it!"

Del swung the old boat into the church parking lot and turned off the motor. She had to think a minute before answering.

"Well," she finally said slowly, "I really don't know. Perhaps God looked all over the universe to find something that was worthy enough to feed our immortal souls, and he didn't find anything. So he gave us himself."

Then she turned to Mara with a smile and said, "Now, that's something to think about, isn't it? Let's go in to Mass!"

38

From Peace to Peaches

At Mass that morning, Mara paid more attention to the prayers and Scripture readings than was customary for her. She found herself really listening to the words of consecration, when Father Mike raised the bread and wine and pronounced those very words that Del had been talking about – "This is my body" and "This is my blood." She glanced at the woman kneeling beside her and after a moment concluded, from the expression on her face, that Del believed what she had told the girl.

At the end of the service, Mara watched as the priest put the leftover bread in that box on the wall. *Tabernacle? I think that's what Del called it. She told me they keep consecrated hosts there to take out to the sick people. And also, so that people can come to pray in the presence of Jesus.*

After every Mass this was where Del always headed for a few minutes of prayer, as she was doing now that everyone else had gone. The girl sat in a pew, watching the play of sunbeams streaming brightly through the multi-colored glass, before she refocused on the woman's head bent in conversation with her Lord.

She sure acts as if Jesus is really there, said the girl to herself. *Could I ever believe that?*

The idea was just too big for the girl to wrap her mind around at this time. Besides, her thoughts kept jumping back her own unfortunate circumstances. What *was* she going to do? Here it was August already and school would be starting in less than a month. Del kept encouraging her to pray for guidance, but Mara could only stumble along in her prayer efforts. She had complained to Del that she couldn't concentrate long enough to pray. The woman said it didn't matter, to keep trying, that God understands and is pleased with our attempts.

She closed her eyes in the quiet of the sunlit church. But once again her past swept over her, engulfing her with dark images and the all-too-familiar feelings of fear, anger and loathing. She squeezed her eyes shut more tightly and her hands flew up to cover her ears to try to block out the screaming inside her memories and the sound of a slap across her face. A heavy weight seemed to nearly suffocate her, just like in her nightmares. Nausea hit her empty stomach, and to calm it she tried taking a few deep breaths before opening her eyes.

Breathing hard and wiping away the beads of perspiration on her forehead, her attention was drawn to Del still in prayer before the tabernacle. As quickly as the brutal thoughts had come, they left her and an empty feeling settled in their place. She walked around inside that emptiness for a moment, then remembered the peacefulness she had felt in that cathedral at Mass. Just the simple act of remembering the peace brought it back to settle like a comforting blanket around her.

Is it true, Jesus, are you really here? Please help me! I don't know what to do about anything in my life.

Del turned around and smiled at her, then came over to ask if she was ready to leave. Mara was mostly quiet on the way home. She was still a little shaky but her stomach settled down after a light lunch. Feeling more like herself, she headed off to the computer to e-mail Peter. She never let on to him where she was, but felt it was safe to tell him about how she was helping to take care of a beautiful garden.

Later that afternoon she and Del were out in that garden, picking some vegetables and giving a drink of water to the plants which had drooped in the heat.

"Be careful," said Del, "don't get water on the leaves or the hot sun might burn them."

Next, Del took over the watering of her beloved hydrangeas. Mara wandered over to check on the progress of the peaches, which had gotten quite large and were starting to show their characteristic rosy blush.

Approaching the fruit tree, the girl startled a large brown squirrel which scurried past her with a stolen peach in its mouth. Mara thought she detected a mischievous glint in its eye when it stopped not far from Del and sat up on its haunches, looking at the woman. Seeing movement out of the corner of her eye, Del noticed the little creature and glowered at the sight of one of her precious peaches clenched in the squirrel's jaw.

"Don't I feed you enough?" she scolded. "What's the matter with you, stealing my peaches! Do you think these things just grow on trees?"

Mara grinned as the squirrel, undisturbed by the lecture, hurried off with its prize.

"Actually," said the woman, turning to her, "I don't mind sharing a little with the critters, even considering all my hard work. But what really gets me is when they take a bite out of one peach, then drop it and go get another! I always remind them they should finish all their food!"

Mara certainly believed that Del would tell the squirrels just what she thought. The girl looked at the ripening peaches and hoped the animals would leave enough of the delicious-looking fruit for them to pick.

She needn't have worried. In a few days the first of the peaches started to ripen, and there were plenty of them. Del showed her how to look for those which had developed a golden-yellow undertone rather than green, and how the peaches' shoulders had a slight give to them, indicating the perfect stage of ripeness. Mara gently picked each ripe peach and laid it carefully in a well-padded basket, first holding its velvety softness to her nose and inhaling deeply its wonderful fragrance.

As with most other produce from the garden, they feasted on what they could eat fresh or baked into goodies, gave some away to neighbors and friends, and froze what was left.

"Nothing like a freshly-thawed bowl of home-grown peaches on a cold winter day to bring back memories of summer," declared Del, peeling away at the sink. "Just wait and see."

At that, the girl working next to her lowered her head. *Wait and see?* she asked herself. *Wait and see how? By winter I should be in school a long way from here, finishing up my senior year.*

Her aching heart really felt torn. She was coming to love it here at Windmill Gardens, yet it wasn't her home. But she couldn't go back to her own home.

What am I going to do? A silent wail tore through her, but Del was busy with the fruit and didn't notice the girl's distress.

39

Corn and Concerns

The first Saturday of August was soon upon them. Once again Del and Mara went with Richard to the city. This time Sean stayed home at his father's insistence to help Ann, so Mara was left on her own to wander the loud and busy farmer's market. She turned a bit pale at the sight of overflowing bushel baskets of peaches. They *used* to be her favorite fruit, she reflected, before she had helped peel hundreds of them. She still enjoyed petting the little animals for sale at the market, and indulged herself with a treat from an ice cream truck parked outside. She made it back to their booth in time to join Del for noon Mass at the cathedral again. She hoped to be invited for another lunch of hamburgers and fries and was not disappointed.

The day ended all too soon, and Mara found herself once more in the back seat of the pickup headed home to Windmill Gardens. Except this time she had her arms wrapped around a kid, of the *goat* variety that is, listening to Richard's assurance that Ann would be absolutely delighted at the addition of a new animal to their farm family. Del looked at her neighbor a bit doubtfully. She inquired whether he didn't think it might have been a better idea to have waited until next year, "what with the new baby coming and everything?"

Richard brushed aside her concerns with a laugh, stating that Ann enjoyed animals as much as he did. Mara wasn't too sure if *she* was all that crazy about this creature right now, as she struggled to keep him quiet by feeding him corn out of her hand.

Just as they turned onto the road leading home, any kind thoughts that she might have had towards the goat dissipated abruptly with the warm drenching of her lap. She dumped the hapless animal onto the floor, yelling and holding her nose, upset even after Richard had apologized and dropped them off at Del's house.

Once she had showered and changed, though, and her smelly, damp clothing was in the washing machine, she calmed down. She helped Del shuck the ears of sweet corn, bought that afternoon at the farmer's market, to boil for their supper.

"Why don't you grow your own corn?" asked Mara, pulling off the long silky strands from the top of a cob.

"I used to," answered Del, "'til I realized that it was too attractive to raccoons. They'd come in for the corn and destroy my fruits and vegetables. One time I even had deer! What a mess! I love animals, but prefer they stay in the woods and out of my garden. So I decided to buy corn and save myself the hassle."

"What's that other bag of corn for that you bought today?" the girl inquired.

"Oh, that's field corn."

"What's the difference?"

"Sweet corn – this stuff here – is higher in sugar and better for eating fresh. Field corn is dried and used for animal feed."

"So, what are *you* going to do with it?" Mara asked, as she finished cleaning her last cob of corn and dropped it into the pot of hot water on the stove.

"Well, on Monday I'll have you help me take off the kernels. Then we'll dry them for squirrel food and clean the cobs to use for jelly."

One would have thought that there was nothing at Del's house that could surprise the girl any more, but she was completely flabbergasted at Del's last statement.

"You make jelly out of *corncobs?*"

"Why, yes, I do. It's one of my customers' favorites at the far…"

Her last words cut off by a shrill ringing from the bedroom, Del hurried to answer the phone. Mara set out plates and silverware, and was putting fruit in the ceramic bowl on the table when Del returned, her eyes brimming with tears.

"That was Mrs. Briggs' daughter," she said, looking devastated. "Esther passed away this morning." As Del turned down the heat under the corn pot and covered it with a lid, she wiped her eyes with the corner of her apron.

"What a wonderful person she was! And a good friend."

In silence, Del finished getting the rest of their supper ready. However, as they ate she told Mara many stories about

Esther Briggs and, by the time the meal was over, Mara felt almost as if she knew the elderly woman.

"At least some of her children and grandchildren were with her when she died," Del said. "The funeral's going to be Wednesday at noon. I told Alice that I'd bring a dish for the luncheon afterward and she was happy about that."

She reflected for a moment.

"I can't believe how long it's been since I saw all Esther's children. You know, even though it'll be sad, I'm looking forward to seeing them again. We had so much fun together years ago."

Del sighed and looked at Mara.

"I don't suppose you'll want to go to the funeral."

Mara shook her head.

"That's okay," Del said. "You'll be fine here by yourself until I get back. I'll try not to be too late."

On Monday, they went through the arduous process of stripping the kernels from the field corncobs and spreading them out on cookie sheets lined with paper towels. The empty red cobs were then cleaned with an old toothbrush under running water and set aside to dry.

"They have to dry well first and that can take a couple of weeks," explained Del. "Then you put them in a pot of boiling water..."

"You dry them and then put them in water? That doesn't make any sense!"

Del chuckled and had to admit the logic in the girl's statement.

"Who knows? There must be a reason behind it." She continued with the explanation. "You boil them for an hour and a half, then strain the juice and go on to make jelly by adding pectin and sugar."

"And what does this corncob jelly taste like?"

Del scrunched up her round face, her dark eyes dancing behind her glasses, as she tried to think how to describe it.

"Well, it's a little like apple jelly. Really! Except there's this beautiful reddish glow to it."

Del chuckled at the dubious look on Mara's face. As they worked together in the hot kitchen chopping vegetables for the funeral luncheon casserole, Del found herself secretly scrutinizing the girl. Del was starting to realize that there was something different about the teenager lately. She couldn't quite put her finger on it, but Del wasn't one to disregard her instincts. Like always, she prayed as she worked and was becoming increasingly troubled by where her thoughts were leading her.

On Tuesday morning they did the usual garden work together, cutting more flowers and herbs to dry in the garage. Del glanced over at the girl often, noticing anew the pale thin face, watching her take frequent rests in the shade of the large tree. Yes, it *was* rather warm and she herself paused for refreshment more often than usual. But there was also the matter of the girl skipping breakfast. And she had been going to bed earlier in the evenings, sometimes as soon as supper was done.

That afternoon Mara went on the computer, stopping every few minutes to play with the gold kitten on her lap. Del sat in her usual place in the living room with shoes off and feet propped up. Her head, eyes closed, was leaning back against the overstuffed chair. With her rosary in her hand, she wasn't dozing this time, but rather praying fervently for wisdom. After an hour she opened her eyes, put her feet down, and with determination went to the doorway of her son's room to speak to the girl.

"Mara," she began, trying to get the girl's attention. When Mara looked at her, she continued, "Child, I am becoming a little concerned about your health. You don't seem to be feeling well these days."

The girl kept staring at Del but didn't say anything.

"Would you mind if I call Ann and have her come down after supper to take a look at you? You know that she's a nurse, and I'd just feel better if I knew you were all right."

The girl was frowning, clearly not enthusiastic about the idea. But in the end, she shrugged and muttered, "Whatever you want," before turning her attention back to the computer screen in front of her.

Del went to her bedroom, shutting the door behind her. She phoned Ann and they had a very long conversation.

40

Tuesday Evening

In the kitchen Del was aimlessly putting away dishes and wiping the table. Then she swept the floor, not even smiling at the kittens who were chasing the broom as she worked her way across the room. She was listening to the low hum of voices coming from behind the closed door of the guest room. When Ann had arrived ten minutes ago, stethoscope in her pocket, Del had apologized for bothering her in this way. But the younger woman had brushed aside the concern with a wave of her hand.

"I really don't mind," she said smiling. "I've been lying around the house so much that it's good to get out for a change. It's been so hot! I was glad to go outside and feel the breeze that sprung up this evening.

"Oh, hi, Mara!" she said to the girl who had just walked into the living room. "And who's this little guy you're holding?"

Ann reached out to scratch the head of Ginger who was nestled in the girl's arms. She suggested that the two of them go into Mara's room where she could take a look at her. The girl, looking none too happy about the whole thing, handed the kitten to Del and led the way.

Now as she worked in the kitchen, Del listened nervously to the rise and fall of voices. When it became silent for a few minutes she tried to turn her mind to prayer, but the voices began again and she lost her train of thought. She finished sweeping and paced around the kitchen, considered going out to the garden then rejected that idea, paced a little more, got herself a drink of water, then just stood looking sightlessly out of the window.

Suddenly there was a scream from the bedroom, a heart-rending shriek, actually, followed by a loud shout.

"NO!" cried Mara's voice, and Del removed her glasses and rubbed her eyes, frowning as she heard, "No – no – NO!" repeated over and over. She heard Ann's softer voice trying to calm the girl, but next there came loud sobs interspersed with the *No's*. Ann finally emerged from the room, closing the bedroom door and looking over at Del with a troubled face.

She motioned to the other woman to follow her out to the front porch, where she pulled the door shut behind them. Even so, they could still hear the distressed sounds coming from inside the house. Ann took a deep breath, unsure of how to begin.

"I was right, wasn't I?" asked Del, although she already knew the answer.

Ann nodded slowly and responded, "You were right, Del. She's pregnant."

She put her hand on Del's arm. "But, Del, you can tell by her reaction that she had no idea. The look on her face was one of shock when she realized what kind of questions I was asking. She must have been so stressed out by what's been going on in her life that she ignored the symptoms. Or she was in denial."

Del was half-listening, her eyes elsewhere and her mind churning over many thoughts.

"Well," she finally said slowly, trying to sort it all out, "it's obvious she didn't run away from home because she was pregnant, since she didn't know it. Something else made her run, but she won't talk about it.

"So I guess," she said, bringing her gaze back to Ann, "that we'll have to deal with the foremost problem, her pregnancy, and hope that everything else will somehow work itself out."

Ann was quiet for a moment, then hesitantly spoke up.

"Del, under most circumstances I'm against abortion, but maybe in this situation…" Her voice trailed off, then she resumed, "I mean, what could be worse than a child having a child?"

At the word "abortion," Del stiffened. As Ann finished giving her opinion, the older woman drew herself up taller and one could just about imagine seeing sparks fly from her eyes.

"Yes!" she asserted in a steely voice that was almost too soft. Ann took a step back from the quiet, controlled anger. "There *is* something worse. And that's *a child killing a child!*"

"Okay, okay." Ann put her hands up in appeasement. "It was just a thought. So what are you going to do?"

Del let her breath out in a deep sigh and seemed to slump inwardly. She brushed loose hair back from her face and responded to the question wearily.

"I don't know. But we'll work it out. With God's help we'll work it out."

She looked distractedly at Ann and thanked her for coming over. As the younger woman, in the later stages of her own pregnancy, climbed awkwardly into her car and drove off, Del went into the house. She rested her back against the closed front door, praying desperately for guidance. After a short time, noticing that the sobs from the bedroom had quieted, she went over and knocked at the door.

"Mara? May I come in?"

There was no answer, so she opened the door. In the yellowish glow of the bedside lamp, she could see the girl sprawled on top the covers with her face turned toward the wall. Del pulled up a chair and sat down.

"Can we talk?"

There was no response, so she pressed on.

"Ann told me that you're pregnant." Still no response, only an occasional soft sob like a hiccup.

"Child, won't you let me help you?" Nothing.

Del didn't know what to do next, but she knew she had to keep trying. Casting about for something to say, she came up with, "You may not think so now, but Peter will be understanding."

The girl's head snapped around. She looked angrily at Del, practically spitting out the words, *"No, he won't!"*

Del was taken aback for a moment, then said in a compassionate voice, "Child, I don't understand what's going on in your life, but I want you to know that I'm going to be here for you. You don't have to go through this alone."

Mara didn't move but tears began to fill her eyes. She whispered so quietly that Del could barely hear her, "I can't have this baby."

Del knew the girl had had quite a shock to her system and needed some time to adjust. She patted Mara's arm.

"Listen, no one has to make any decisions tonight. We can talk about it tomorrow. I believe I can help you. Now, why don't you try to get some sleep?"

The girl didn't look at her, but shook her head when Del asked if she could get her anything. Del left the bedroom and went to lock up, pulling down shades and turning off lights. Then she picked up her Bible and her rosary and went to her own room. She had a feeling that it would be a very long night.

41

Dilemmas and Decisions

Del was in a dilemma. She had overslept that morning, having spent a great part of the night tossing and turning. At first she had been unable to sleep at all, and then she had fallen into a fitful unrest with last night's conversations still running through her mind. Right now, though, she was dressed and had eaten some breakfast.

Yet she still felt so bleary-minded. Richard had just called, offering to pick her up for the funeral, and she had agreed without thinking. But seated at the kitchen table, staring at the garden flowers rippling in the brisk breeze, she was unable to make up her mind what to do.

She *needed* to go to the funeral, she was sure of that. She owed it to Esther for her kindness and generosity to Del's family. Besides, she had promised Alice that she would be there. But she also *needed* to be at home right now with Mara, with whom she had promised to talk today. Back and forth she went, just like the flowers blowing in the wind outside.

She opened her Bible, pushed up her glasses and rubbed her tired eyes before beginning to read. She found great comfort and hope in Psalm 23, believing that the Lord really *was* her shepherd and would lead her along the right paths. By the time she finished the psalm, she decided to leave Mara in God's capable hands and go to the funeral. Besides, she reasoned, she would not be gone all that long and could talk with her when she came home.

When Richard pulled into the driveway and beeped his horn, Del went and knocked at the bedroom door. When there was no answer she opened it wide enough to poke her head in. The girl turned toward her and Del saw eyes which were red-rimmed and puffy.

Looks like she didn't sleep either, thought Del, but all she said was, "Are you all right?"

The girl nodded slightly and Del continued, "I have to go to that funeral. I hope I won't be too long. There's some sandwiches for you in the fridge. Please try to eat something. We'll talk when I get home, okay?"

Mara nodded again, so Del went to get her casserole from the kitchen. She pulled the front door shut behind her and it locked with a loud click.

The girl heard the door close and the pickup drive away. Then there was nothing but silence. She just lay there sprawled on top of the covers, staring at the ceiling and trying not to think. The shadows on the walls changed slowly as noontide passed and the afternoon began.

Hunger finally drove her to the kitchen, where she munched on a sandwich and stared out the window vacantly. Numbly she shuffled to the refrigerator to pour herself a glass of milk. The kittens jumped out of their box, expecting to play. But, unlike her usual self, she barely paid them any attention. Finally making up her mind to take a shower, she went to her room to look through her sparse collection of clothing. Pulling out some clean blue jeans and a plaid shirt that had belonged to Del's son, she headed off for a shower which she hoped would help clear her mind.

A little while later she was at the table again, her hair clumped in damp strands around her face and her shirt hanging out half-unbuttoned. She sat there for the longest time with her head in her hands, trying to suppress the thoughts that kept coming at her like little bullets of pain shooting into her memory. Last night the well-known nightmares had once again been back to haunt her restless sleep. They brought with them reminders of her last days at home which she had tried so hard to forget.

She shook her head several times, but couldn't shake the hopelessness of her situation. No matter which way she tried turning, she would run into a wall with no doors. *Don't think, don't think, don't think...*

For nearly an hour she struggled to keep the darkness away, when suddenly she was startled by Mama Cat rubbing against her leg. Glancing down at the animal, Del's words sprang into her mind. *Would I have taken you in if I'd known you were pregnant?*

Tears filled Mara's eyes as she leaned on the table and cradled her head on her folded arms. For the longest time, anguish and confusion filled her heart, tearing at her and cutting her into little pieces. A piece here and a piece there, not knowing where she belonged and lacking hope of *ever* belonging.

It was in a desperate attempt to put those pieces back together again that she finally made up her mind what she needed to do. Pushing her hair back with one hand, she raised her head but kept her eyes away from the tranquil garden, the garden of peace, that could be seen through the window. She used the sleeve of her shirt to wipe the tears from her face, and with that gesture resolutely wiped away all thought except the task ahead of her.

It was three o'clock when Mara scrounged up a pencil and a piece of paper, wrote a short note and taped it to her bedroom door. She went to the kitchen cupboard where the phone directories were kept and took down the big one for the city. Standing at the kitchen table, she pushed aside Del's Bible and set down the phone book, thumbing through the pages until she found what she was looking for. Her eyes preoccupied with scanning the ads, she buttoned up her shirt and absent-mindedly tucked it into her jeans. Then, tearing out the page, she closed the book and picked it up before stepping away from the table to return it to its shelf.

Unfortunately however, and unbeknownst to the girl, the hanging end of the linen runner on the table had inadvertently gotten tucked into her waistband with her shirt. When she turned and walked away with the phone book, the runner was pulled off the table and the ceramic fruit bowl fell with a loud *crash!*

Mara jumped, spinning around quickly. Her eyes flew wide open and her face blanched. On the kitchen floor lay the bowl, broken in several pieces. And worse, partially under one of the pieces, was a little gold-furred form lying absolutely still.

An agonized cry – *"Ginger!"* – tore through the empty house and echoed off the walls. Mara, dropping the phone book and diving for the kitten, threw the bowl aside and lifted the tiny broken body onto the palm of her hand where its paws dangled limply. Cross-legged, she sat on the floor, groaning and sobbing and holding the kitten to her chest. She rocked back and forth, willing with all her strength to undo the damage she had caused.

Fresh anguish wracked her as she stroked the soft fur and remembered the kitten chasing after a string, cuddling up under her chin or climbing determinedly up her pant leg with its little claws. She touched the soft, still paws and thought about how

Ginger would stalk the other kittens and pounce on them, and they would roll over and over each other in a tangle of feet and fur. Her hot tears kept falling on the gold fuzz, turning it to a darker shade where they landed, as she laid the body of the kitten in her lap and cried and cried, her body heaving with sobs.

At long last, with tears still streaming down her face, she woodenly gathered up the pieces of broken bowl. Taking them, along with the dead kitten, outside to the garden, she laid everything behind a bush close to the garage. She returned to the kitchen, put away the phone book after tucking the torn-out page into her pocket, and went to her room to stuff her belongings into her backpack. Closing the bedroom door behind her, she stood for a minute in the living room, wiping her tear-streaked face while trying to think. Then she went to the other bedroom, and picked up the credit card that Del had left lying next to the computer. Backpack in hand, Mara hurried into the back room and lifted the car keys off their hook before heading to the garage.

She put up the garage door, backed the car out and then, as Del always did, waited for a moment to watch the door swing down. The girl glanced around at the house, the yard and the giant mailbox. But it was when she saw the circle of windmill blades as they turned slowly in the breeze high over the garage roof that her heart was pierced with a sudden, sharp ache. Quickly she closed down all thought and forced herself to begin the long drive to the city.

42

Late Wednesday

There was a lot of fussing and fuming going on in Del's thoughts. She was finally on her way home, listening inattentively to the chatter of the woman who was driving, but for her there was only one subject – Mara.

I shouldn't have left her, she kept saying to herself. *I didn't know I'd be gone so long.* She glanced at her watch. *It's after five o'clock!*

The trouble had begun at the end of the funeral Mass. Father Mike had ended the service with an invitation to Esther's children, some of whom had had their flights delayed and didn't arrive until that morning, to come up and say a few words about their mother. Well, none of them was able to resist telling just one more story. As time passed she could feel Richard, seated next to her, getting fidgety.

Earlier on the ride into town, he had told her that Ann was experiencing back pain. So now, while the deceased's family was eulogizing, he decided to slip over to the nearby party store and give his wife a call. When he returned, clambering into the pew over the legs of several people, he whispered to Del that Ann was having contractions. Del knew he was concerned since there were still three or four weeks to go until the due date. She whispered back that he should go home, that she'd be able to find a ride and he needn't worry.

At the luncheon at the Briggs' homestead, there were so many people to visit with – Esther's family, old friends and townspeople – that time seemed to fly by. Dear old Louise, a long-time acquaintance from church, had cheerfully offered to give Del a ride home. But as the afternoon dragged on, Del was a bit more pointed about it and told Louise that she really needed to go.

"Oh, sure!" agreed Louise, amiably. "Let's make our goodbyes and I'll run you on home."

But Del's goodbyes, with Mara on her mind, were much shorter than Louise's goodbyes, which were just one more reason to start up a conversation with yet another person. Del waited near the door, her empty dish in her hands, shifting restlessly from one foot to another.

Loquacious Louise! she fumed interiorly, trying not to appear too agitated. Del was generally not an unkind person, even in her thoughts, but this was really too much to take when there was something vitally important going on at home. *Patience, Del, patience,* she tried counseling herself without much success. Then, *Lord, could you please light a fire under Louise?*

It was late in the afternoon when they were finally on their way. Although Del was really irritated and found it wearisome to listen to the woman's ceaseless chatter, Louise didn't seem to notice. After being dropped off in her own driveway, Del thanked her and heaved a big sigh as the other woman drove away.

She let herself into the house and stood there a moment, listening. *It's so quiet,* she thought, and called out, "Mara?"

No answer. She spied a small piece of paper taped to Mara's door and walked over with some trepidation. She let her breath out in relief as she read, "I was tired so I went to bed early."

Best thing for the girl. I can talk to her tomorrow.

Del went to the kitchen and set her dish to soak in the sink before opening the refrigerator. She was happy to note that one of the sandwiches she'd left for Mara had been eaten, so she took out the other for her own supper. She really wasn't very hungry, but she was *extremely* weary. If she hadn't been so tired maybe she would have noticed that the fruit bowl was missing from the table. But she just stared out the window as she ate, noticing that there were a few things that needed to be done in the garden after supper.

When the chores were finished and the house was locked up for the night, she went to her own bedroom to retire early. For as long as she could keep her bleary eyes open, she prayed for God's grace and mercy for her young troubled friend, and for the words that she would need to say tomorrow. If Del had known that Mara was not safe and sound in the other bedroom, she would never have drifted off to sleep so quickly.

43

The Second Day

Her morning prayers were finished and the gardening chores were underway. At least Del had slept better than she had the previous night. With a good night's sleep, even the worst of circumstances could be approached with more optimism. The time she had spent with the Lord earlier at the kitchen table clarified in her mind what needed to be said to the girl today. Now, as she worked with her hands in the garden, she prayed in her heart for the courage to say it.

At midmorning, she went into the house and called the Spencer farm to find out how Ann was doing. Sean answered the phone and said that his mom was resting, that the contractions had stopped for the moment but the doctor had ordered her to stay in bed. Did she want to talk to his dad?

Since Richard was out in the barn, Del said, "No, just tell him I called and to let me know if he needs anything." Then she made breakfast and knocked on Mara's door. No answer, as she had expected. She knocked again, more loudly this time.

"Mara? Do you want some breakfast?"

When there was still no sound from within the room, Del opened the door part way and peered around it.

"What…?!"

Where was she? Del flipped on the light switch to see better. She quickly scanned the room, first the rumpled bed and then the open closet and the corners of the room, as if somehow expecting that Mara was just hiding somewhere, waiting to jump out and yell, "Fooled ya!"

She looked in the bathroom and the computer room, but no Mara. Returning to the guest bedroom, she searched for the girl's backpack and purse, but they were nowhere to be found. Del stood in the middle of the living room, panic rising in her throat. *Where could she have gone?* She thought to check the front door, but it was still locked securely. She even went out in the backyard and looked around the garden, while sheepishly admitting to herself that it was unlikely that the girl was out there and somehow escaped her notice.

She returned to the kitchen and sat down heavily in a chair. Her heart pounding, she tried to bring some sense to her scattered thoughts and feelings. *Take a deep breath, Del. That's it, just keep breathing slowly and try to calm down. Oh, my Lord, whatever has happened to that child?*

Del gave herself a minute to settle her agitated mind, then made an attempt to look at the situation in a logical manner. *Let's see, she was here last night. She went to bed early because she was tired. Could she have slipped out during the night and run off into the woods again? Maybe I shouldn't have taught her those wilding skills. Now she thinks she can survive in the wilderness!*

But Del knew immediately that that was a foolish thought. In the past few weeks the girl had shown little interest in what Del could teach her, spending all her free time on the computer. *Could she have made contact through the internet with someone who came to get her?* But Del was sure she would have heard Mara leave during the night. The doors were locked and the girl would have had to close them rather forcefully to re-lock behind her.

Then Del remembered the note taped to the bedroom door last night. *Maybe that was to throw me off track, and she was already gone by the time I got home yesterday.* The more she thought about it, the more that made sense. Del became upset with herself.

Why, oh, why didn't I think about checking on her when I got home?

But Del finally came to the realization that all that was water under the bridge. The more pressing problem was what to do now. For the longest time, she sat thinking and thinking, trying to pray but not succeeding very well. Finally her growling stomach got her attention, and she spooned out some of the cooked oatmeal for lunch that she had intended to eat for breakfast.

It was while she was eating that she noticed that the ceramic bowl which had been on the table was gone. Confused, she tried to think. *Wasn't it sitting right here yesterday? Was it here last night when I came home? I just can't remember!* She glanced over at the counter and seeing it wasn't there either, she searched through the kitchen cupboards and the back room.

Now where could that have gone to? First the girl, then the bowl – how strange!

Del hadn't yet noticed that Ginger was also missing. If she hadn't been so preoccupied, she might have wondered why Mama Cat seemed unsettled and very unlike herself, prowling about the house as if looking for something which was lost. The cat finally crouched down by Del's feet, meowing mournfully, and the woman absent-mindedly patted Mama and went to pour cat food into the bowl. She sat down again before Coco and Pepper scampered over to sniff at the food their mother was eating.

Del's heart felt as if it was breaking, but she shook her head, rubbed her eyes and determined to keep herself busy in the garden after lunch. How many times in the past had she found comfort and answers while working among the beautiful flowers?

But she never made it out to the garden. As she was passing through the back room, she happened to notice that the car keys weren't hanging in their usual place. After pausing a moment, trying to remember if perhaps she had put them in her purse, a sudden sinking feeling hit her like a ton of bricks. She flung open the door to the garage and stood there looking helplessly at the place where her car should have been.

Del was incredulous. *How could she take my car?! She knows that's my only transportation!* Very upset, she threw up her hands and kept talking to herself, still nonplussed as she went back to the kitchen. Del was certain now that the girl had left some time yesterday while she was at the funeral. Pausing by the table, she saw the cats milling around the food dish and, even in her agitation, noticed that the little gold kitten wasn't there. Baffled, she searched everywhere in the house, even getting her plump body down on all fours to peer into the cat's box under the table.

She heaved herself back to her feet. *I can't believe it. She must have taken Ginger, too!*

Del dropped into one of the kitchen chairs and felt like crying. What a mess this all was! What was she going to do now? Report her car as stolen? *Then I'll have to tell the whole story about the girl!* Del wondered if her insurance company would even consider the car stolen if they knew she'd given Mara permission to drive it. *And I don't have money to buy another car! Good grief, I haven't even paid off the last repair bills on this one!*

Overriding every other concern, though, was where the girl had gone. *To search for her father? She doesn't know where he's living, but maybe the distress of finding out she's pregnant made her grab at straws.* Then Del wondered if maybe Mara had decided to tell Peter about her pregnancy and he had talked her into meeting him somewhere.

As the thoughts kept whirling around, Del sat dejectedly at the table. She was so distraught, in fact, that she didn't go to the living room for her usual afternoon prayer. And that's when the Deceiver took the opportunity to come again. This time he brought along his fellow demons, Self-righteousness and Bitterness, speaking so softly to her in her own voice that she didn't realize the deception.

How could that girl have done this to me? Del was starting to get angry. *Look at all I did for her and she took advantage of me!*

Del became so agitated that even her usual kindness left her. Resentment reared his ugly head, whispering in her ear.

That little brat! She took everything she could get. She's so selfish she can't think of anyone but herself. As if no one else has problems!

Del thought of Ann's warnings the first night the girl arrived, and Embarrassment swarmed around her. *How naïve I was! Treating the girl like my own daughter! How could I have been so dumb?*

Fear and Indecision arrived next. *I should have called the authorities right away. Am I going to get in trouble for not reporting a runaway? I wish I could call Richard for some advice, but he's got his hands full right now. Oh, whatever should I do?*

She became so upset that, if Mara had walked into the room at that moment, Del would have wrung her neck. Flinging herself out of her chair, she hurried through the house and threw open the front door. She marched out to where the mailbox stood, shaded her eyes and peered down the road, all the time berating herself for being so stupid as to think that the girl was just going to take it into her head to come back.

As she returned to the house and stalked back through the living room, complaining loudly and angrily to herself, she came to an abrupt halt. There, on the wall right in front of her eyes, was the crucifix.

Suddenly, she felt ashamed. All her fussing and whining and resentment, and here on the cross was the One who had borne every evil without murmuring. Tears of sorrow sprang to her eyes and she prayed the words that she always said, when she couldn't get past her human feelings to even begin to see things from God's point of view.

> *Oh, my Jesus,*
> *Take away my feelings and give me your feelings.*
> *Take away my thoughts and give me your thoughts.*
> *Take away my desires and give me your desires.*
> *Take my will and conform it entirely to yours.*

She said it again, over and over many times, until at last she could feel the hurt and resentment melt away, and the black cloud that had been hovering over her head disappeared. The Deceiver had been vanquished for the time being. The only thing remaining was concern for the girl's welfare. And she continued to take that concern to the heart of her Savior as she went back reluctantly to her interrupted work outside.

Throughout the rest of the day, she stopped her chores every so often to hurry out to the road and gaze down it a long ways. *I will keep watching and waiting,* she told herself firmly, *until the Lord himself gives me reason to do otherwise.*

It seemed to be a coincidence that evening when Del decided to do a little garden work directly behind the garage, and a flash of a light color behind a bush caught her eye. No one else would ever have noticed it, but the woman was intimately familiar with her garden and she knew that something looked out of place.

She knelt down, dragged out a piece of her ceramic bowl and stared at it, trying to figure out how it had broken and why it was here. Then she pulled out another piece, and another. At last, the body of the dead kitten was exposed. With a heavy heart, Del went to get a shovel from the garage and she buried Ginger under the lilac bush next to the windmill.

Is this why you left, child? It must have been an accident which killed the kitten. Did you run away because of this? Or was it just the final straw?

Daylight was fading rapidly, but broken-hearted Del stood there for quite some time in the beautiful garden, leaning heavily on her shovel. Tears streaming down her face, she cried for Mara and for Ginger, and she cried at the memory of another girl long ago who had run away after an accident.

44

Prodigal

On the morning of the third day, Del abruptly sat up in bed. She had been tossing fitfully most of the night and only a few hours had passed since she had finally dropped off to sleep. But now a clear thought struck her, arousing her from her restless dreams. Now she *knew* where the girl had gone.

Sticking her feet into fuzzy green slippers, she shuffled her way to the kitchen cupboard where she took down the phone directory and flipped to the "A" section. There was a page that had been torn out, and when Del saw that it was the one with listings for abortion clinics, she sank down slowly into her chair with her hand pressed tightly over her mouth. *Oh, God, have mercy, have mercy!* she cried silently, the missing page confirming what she already knew in her heart.

She put her head down on her folded arms and spent the morning sitting there in agony, unable to do anything but pray. Finally, she shook off her stupor, got dressed, and then went out to stand by the road. Shortly after the noon hour, she saw a small cloud of dust working its way quickly down the dirt road. Her heart leaped, but she was disappointed at last to see only the mail carrier's car as it stopped at the Spencer's mailbox. She went into the house then, having no desire to pass the time of day with anyone at that moment, and fixed herself something quick to eat. After the mail carrier had come and gone, she went out to wait by the mailbox again, not even thinking to check what was in it.

Several times she returned to the house but seemed unable to accomplish the simplest task. Before long, she would be out in front again, keeping what would seem to anyone else a desperate vigil. But Del was a woman who knew the virtue of hope, which sprang naturally like an irrepressible stream flowing from the fountain of her ongoing prayer.

It was late that afternoon when far, far off down the road, Del saw another, smaller cloud of dust being raised by a vehicle traveling at a much slower pace than the mail carrier's had been. She watched as the tiny speck got a little closer, but it seemed to come to a halt even before reaching the Spencer farm. She squinted in the bright afternoon sunshine but couldn't make out anything except that it had definitely stopped moving.

Inspired with an idea, she ran as fast as her short legs would carry her into the house, yanked the binoculars off their hook and scurried back out to the road. Holding them to her eyes and adjusting the focus, she could finally make out that the speck was certainly an automobile, and it was – was it? – yes, it did seem to be green!

Back into the house she went, threw the binoculars on the couch, ran through the back room and into the garage, hit the "up" button for the garage door and wheeled out a dusty old ten-speed bike that had belonged to her son. No matter that the tires were a bit flat, or that she had a great deal of trouble getting on the tall bike. After a couple of false starts and balancing awkwardly on the high seat, she managed to get it moving. It wobbled a little unsteadily as she began to make her way down the road. Faster and faster she pedaled, her breath coming in hard gasps and her heart pounding faster than pistons in a motor.

The sight of the woman bent over the handlebars and pumping furiously on the pedals, her face red and perspiring and her hair loosening from its pins, with her too-large shirt billowing out behind her, was strange indeed. But Del was concerned with nothing but that little dot on the horizon, growing larger as she drew closer.

She flew past the Spencer farm where Sean and Abby were playing in the front yard. They ran out to the road to get a closer look as the woman buzzed by, quite astonished at this rare spectacle.

Soon Del could make out the front of a car – her car! – which gave her reason to demand even more from her aching legs, and she quickly drew alongside it. Skidding on the gravel road by the driver's door, she nearly killed herself trying to stop the bike and dismount all at once. Leaving the bike where it had fallen in the middle of the road, she yanked open the car door.

Mara had her head leaning against the top of the steering wheel, and now, startled, she looked up with a tear-streaked face.

But Del gave her no chance to say anything. She squeezed her ample body into the front seat next to the girl and threw her arms tightly around her. Rocking a little back and forth, as one would comfort a distressed child, she just held Mara who was sobbing her heart out, and cried right along with her.

For a long time they sat intertwined in the crowded seat, until the girl's crying had lessened into occasional hiccups. Dropping her arms and leaning back to place her hand under the girl's chin, Del searched the anguished face in front of her.

"Mara, Mara, Mara," she pleaded in a gentle voice. "Child, what have you done?"

But either the girl didn't understand what she meant or chose not to, because with fresh tears she cried out in a strangled voice, "Ginger!"

Del hugged her again, stroking her hair and saying, "Child, that was just an accident! It was just an accident!"

It was just an accident.

Her aunt's words of long ago echoed and resounded through her mind. In that moment, Mercy given became Mercy received, as Del felt within herself the final cracking away of something which had lain encrusted around her own heart for far too long.

She continued to hold the girl, waiting for the storm of emotions to subside, until at last Mara sat up straighter and said in a sorrowful tone, "Oh, Del, I took your car!" She looked as if she might cry again.

"Hush," declared Del through her own tears. "It doesn't matter. You're back now. Why don't we go home?"

Del got out of the car, picked up the bike and stuffed it as well as she could into the roomy trunk. With the bike's front wheel dangling and the trunk lid bouncing freely up and down, she drove slowly down the road towards Windmill Gardens. Passing the Spencer farm, she waved and shouted out the open window at the surprised children, "She's come back! Mara's home again!"

45

Tragic Tale

Del flitted nervously about the kitchen making sure that the girl had some nourishing food in her stomach. After eating, Mara asked if she could take a shower. That was fine with Del, as it gave her time to sit in the easy chair and collect her thoughts. She told Mara that they were going to talk as soon as she came out, and the girl nodded. So Del waited in the silence, thanking God for the prodigal's return and praying for guidance about what would happen next.

Mara finally emerged, her hair damp and her face scrubbed. Her eyes were still red, and she rubbed them with her hand as she flopped down on the couch. When the woman didn't say anything, the girl took a deep breath and in a barely audible voice said, "I'm sorry."

Del just looked at her sympathetically, which encouraged the girl to continue.

"I shouldn't have taken your car. After all you've done for me! I mean, taking me in off the streets..."

A hint of a smile touched Del's lips, and the girl corrected herself.

"Okay, the woods, then."

Mara stared vacantly at the floor.

"I didn't know what else to do. I was so upset and scared over everything going on." Tears began to well in her eyes again. "Can you ever forgive me?"

Del went over to the couch to sit next to the girl and put her arm around her.

"Of course," she asserted quietly, "I forgive you. There's nothing you can do that will ever make me stop loving you. And you know something else?"

The woman removed her arm from the girl's shoulders and with her hand lifted up Mara's face.

"There's also nothing you can do that will ever make *God* stop loving you. He not only loves you, he will forgive anything you've done..." Del paused a moment and sighed, "...even an abortion."

The girl looked startled, her eyes opening wider, perhaps not having realized that Del had known. She quickly turned her head away and her hair screened her face. They sat there for a few moments in silence. Then the girl said so softly that Del could barely hear her, "I didn't have an abortion."

Del was a little stunned, but just said, "Child, why don't you tell me everything, starting from when I left the house to go to the funeral?"

So Mara, in a halting voice, told Del what had happened to the kitten, and how she had fled to the city to look for one of the abortion clinics listed in the phone directory. But everything had gone wrong. She had gotten lost in the endless maze of one-way streets and, by the time she arrived, the clinic was closed for the day. She had driven around for awhile but couldn't find any of the other places.

Furthermore, she was in a rather rundown part of the city. She locked the car doors and kept driving aimlessly, then realized how hungry she was. After she stopped at a fast-food restaurant it was getting dark, so she pulled into the parking lot of an industrial building and slept in the car. At that Del shuddered a little, thinking of all the things that could have happened to the child alone in the city at night.

The next day Mara tried to find her way back to the same clinic and had gotten lost several times. She realized she was running low on gas and stopped to get some, picked up a sandwich at a convenience store and at last arrived at the clinic some time in the afternoon.

"I sat in the car for the longest time. But I finally went in, and had to fill out a form with my name and address. I just made up stuff and wrote it down and they didn't ask me any questions about it. They even believed me when I put down that I was eighteen. They asked me how I was going to pay and I gave them your credit card." The girl looked embarrassed.

My credit card? Del tried not to look surprised, but simply nodded for the girl to continue.

"So this lady took me into another room, told me to take off my clothes and put on this ugly gown, and I was starting to get

159

really nervous. I was sitting there waiting when she came back in and told me there was a problem with the credit card. They wouldn't take it! Said it was already up to its 'credit limit'."

At that, Del let out her breath, not even realizing that she had been holding it. If the situation hadn't been so serious, she might have chuckled. *All those car repairs in May,* she thought, remembering her frustration at the time with how much money she was spending on that old thing. *I wasn't so thankful at the time, but I thank you now, Lord.*

The girl, unaware of the thoughts going through Del's mind, went on.

"They wanted to know if I had any cash, but I had barely enough to buy a hamburger for dinner. They told me I should come back when I had enough money."

She stopped, looking as if she was going to cry again.

"I got dressed and ran out of there in a panic and took off. I didn't realize where I was driving, but I didn't really care. Suddenly I recognized the area I was in – it was near the farmer's market – then I saw the cathedral and pulled into its parking lot."

Del went to get a glass of water for the girl. This hot August evening was stifling, and Mara was perspiring and looked exhausted. After drinking it, she continued her tale in a rush of words, not looking at Del who sat down next to her again.

"I just stayed in the car. I was so mixed up and didn't know what to do. But looking up at the church's spires against the evening sky somehow made me feel a little better. Maybe I even said a prayer. I don't know. I slept there in the car last night, and when this morning came I was able to go into the cathedral to use the bathroom. And then on the way out, when I was going down the steps, there was that old priest. You know – the one who said Mass? He was coming up the steps, and he smiled at me and said, 'Good morning, child.' And that got me thinking about you, about maybe coming back here. But it took me all day to work up the courage to do it."

The girl sniffled and glanced at the woman before looking away quickly. All Del could think of to say was, "I'm glad you did."

"But, Del," the girl sniffled again, "what am I going to do?!" Her words were pleading and challenging at the same time as she repeated her words of several days ago, "I *can't* have this baby!"

Del wiped the back of her hand across her forehead, trying to think and pray at the same time. She had listened and now felt it was time to give some advice.

"Child," she began, "problems have to be faced. They can't be run away from. Believe me, I tried when I was young to do just that. And I promise you that I will do everything in my power to help you. But you have to tell me some things. First of all, was it Peter who got you pregnant?"

"Peter!" The name practically exploded from the girl's lips, and now she was angry. "I told you, Pete is a *friend!"*

Del was a bit nonplussed by this outburst, but she forged ahead nonetheless.

"All right," she said soothingly. "If it wasn't Peter, then who was it?"

The girl's agitation increased.

"It *wasn't* Peter," she yelled, "it was *Tom!"* She spit out the name and began to wail.

Tom? Del was puzzled, remembering that that was the name which had caused Mara, weeks earlier, to be so fearful. There was nothing to do now but insist on the whole story.

"Okay, Mara, the only way I can help you is if you'll be honest with me about what's happened."

Sobbing, Mara shook her head, but Del kept asking questions until she got the truth out of the girl piece by piece. It turned out that Tom was her mother's boyfriend. Since he had moved into their home several years ago, Mara had tried hard to stay out of his way. He got drunk a lot and when he was drinking he was abusive. And not long ago he had started to crawl in bed with Mara.

Now Del was angry, but she held her tongue and prodded the girl to go on.

"My mother is a waitress, and sometimes she has to work evenings, so I'd put my little sister down to sleep. It was on one of those nights that he first started getting into bed with me and...and touching me." Mara started stammering, her voice shaking.

"And...and the first few times I...I was able to slip away from him because he was so drunk, but then he...then he started to threaten me. He said if I told he'd k-kill me. And I think he really would! I ran away from home after he... after he..." The girl was too upset to finish.

Del moved closer and wrapped her arms around her.

"Okay, okay, I get the picture. You don't need to go on."

She waited while Mara cried herself out on Del's shoulder, although Del was so angry she wanted to cry too.

How could anyone do this to a child? Why, oh why, Lord, does she have to bear so much? And how am I going to help her?

After a few minutes, she held the girl away from her and said, "Child, look at me."

Mara reluctantly brought her tearful gaze up to Del's face.

The woman continued, "I have promised to help you, and I will. But I have to ask you – did you ever tell your mother?"

The girl narrowed her gaze and looked away.

"I was afraid to at first, because he was threatening me. But I finally did. At least...I tried."   ·

"And what did she say?"

"She slapped me. And told me to stop lying."

Her own mother! Del, who saw the whole world through the eyes of a mother, was extremely pained by the betrayal and abandonment this child must have felt. But now, looking at Mara's exhausted face, she realized that there was nothing else that needed to be said tonight, so she sent the girl off to bed.

Del sat there for quite awhile, unable to move as thoughts and emotions spun about in her head. She finally got her aching legs underneath her and launched herself towards her own room to pray and then try to get some sleep.

Help me, Lord, to say tomorrow what I must say but don't want to.

46

Confessions

Del had felt so drained the previous evening that she intended to sleep a little later the next morning. But she still woke early, her mind already in gear. The more she lay there, pondering Mara's situation, the angrier she became. Angry at the man who had taken advantage of a helpless teenager, and angry at the mother who had failed to believe or help her own child. Del was just as angry at the clinic workers, who hadn't cared enough about a young desperate girl walking through their doors to try to find out why she was in such a predicament. Del was certain that an abortion was not going to help Mara. The girl had been raped! An abortion would just eliminate the evidence and, for all that clinic knew, she could be going back into the same abusive situation.

Still upset, Del managed to get out of bed, even though every joint ached when she moved. A warm shower helped ease some of the pain and also cleared her head a bit. She came to realize that anger wasn't going to solve anything. What she needed now were the right words to say. So after her shower, she sat in her usual place at the kitchen table and opened her prayer book to the Psalm of the Day:

> "I wait for you, O Lord; I lift up my soul to my God. In
> you I trust…Guide me in your truth and teach me, for you
> are God my Savior…Relieve the troubles of my heart,
> bring me out of my distress."

Well, that's appropriate, she thought. *Dearest Lord, I ask this day for your help for Mara and guidance for me.* Del prayed a long time, ignoring even the morning chores that needed doing in the garden outside her window. At last, she heard the girl getting up and she quickly made pancakes for breakfast.

Previously, Mara hadn't had much appetite in the morning, but she ate more today than usual. She didn't look quite so depressed, either, and Del reflected that the sharing of one's problems often helps relieve the burden a bit. Determined not to wait to tackle the subject, after clearing the dishes she asked the girl to sit with her at the table so they could talk.

However, the girl jumped in before Del had a chance to open her mouth.

"Del," she stated quietly but with determination in her voice, "I have to have an abortion. I *hate* that man. I can't even imagine having his child."

Del was sympathetic. "I know, child, this whole situation is totally awful. I don't blame you for feeling that way. But a decision doesn't have to be made right this minute."

She was silent a moment, then touched the arm of the girl.

"Mara, I've thought of something. In the next town there's a place with wonderful people who help girls like yourself who are in the same situation you are. They can guide you through any difficulty you have, and *I* will help you, too."

"Do they do abortions?" the girl demanded.

"No, they don't. But there's something I want you to think about. That baby that's growing inside you is also *your* child. Even though you can't feel it, he or she already has a heartbeat, and is totally dependent upon you for everything – nourishment, warmth and a safe place to grow.

"Yes," she continued, "what happened to you is more than abuse. You were raped. And rape is certainly an act of violence against an innocent person. But *abortion* is also an act of violence. It destroys an innocent baby. An abortion isn't going to solve your problems. It'll only add to them."

As Del talked, the girl got more upset and shouted angrily at her, "How do *you* know?"

Del looked out the window. She knew it had been coming, but she was still unprepared to talk about it. However there was nothing to be done but plunge ahead.

"I know that abortion's not the answer," she asserted quietly, pulling her gaze back to the girl, "because I *had* an abortion many years ago." She stopped and took a deep breath before saying, "Actually, I had *two* abortions." When she told Mara the dates they had taken place, the girl gave her a strange look. But Del went on without stopping to take a breath.

"I told you how I had run away, and that I had gotten mixed up in a bad lifestyle. Too many parties, too much drinking, and before I knew it I found out I was pregnant. Well, I was determined not to have a baby, especially since I barely knew the guy and he wasn't someone I wanted to be linked to the rest of my life. Abortion wasn't legal at the time, but I found someone to do it. The guy's office was gross. I felt sick just walking in there. It's a wonder I didn't get an infection or something. And I felt horrible afterwards. Oh, maybe on the surface I was relieved for a while. But looking back at it, I realize that, even then, I knew I had killed my own child."

Del paused. Her face was flushed and her heart was pounding loudly in her ears. She didn't know if she could go on, but she had to finish the story for Mara's sake.

"And I can't say it was anything more than a temporary solution. Because I still had the same problems, maybe even more, and within a short time I was pregnant again. I went back for another abortion. It had just become legal, but it was the same abortionist. His place might've been a little cleaner, but no one there cared about what I was going through. It was in and out, take my money and that was it. And my second child died."

Suddenly, Del thought about the words of Mother Teresa, the little nun who worked among the poorest of the poor in India. *She said it was a very great poverty that a child should die so that we may live as we wish. I certainly lived as I wished, and now I'd give anything if I could turn back time and have my children here with me.*

Her thoughts were interrupted by the girl asking, "Is that what those painted stones are for in your garden?"

Del nodded.

"As I said before, I met Joe, we got married and I had more children. I tried to keep busy, but deep inside I realized the horror of what I'd done. When I went to confession like I told you, I was finally able to find some peace. There was a very wise priest there. He not only assured me of God's forgiveness, he advised me to name the babies that I had aborted. As I prayed about it, the names 'Rose' and 'Veronica' came to mind. Eventually I realized that those were names of flowers, so I put a rose and a Veronica plant in my garden and painted the rocks to go next to them."

She looked out in that direction across the backyard, although the garden with the painted rocks was hardly visible from the window. Her voice dropped to a near whisper.

"It's my constant reminder that God in his merciful love has forgiven me, and because he has, I can forgive myself. I really believe that he sent that youth group and my future husband into the city streets to find me. He's a good shepherd in that way," said Del sadly but with a small smile on her face, "always searching for the lost sheep."

Mara didn't smile.

"But you said that God would forgive me, too, if I have an abortion."

"That's true," Del countered, "but you certainly can't presume on his mercy, by going ahead and doing something you *know* is wrong. And there's not a woman on this earth who doesn't know in her heart – however much she may deny it – that it's wrong to take the life of her own child. Believe me, abortion may seem like the only answer, but the anguish from it goes on forever…"

Del was going to say more, but the girl pressed forcefully on, resentment in her voice.

"I still can't imagine having a baby that's *his*."

"I know, child. But Mara," Del said as a sudden thought struck her, "who is the father of your little sister?"

The girl didn't say anything. She just lowered her eyes in silence and Del knew the answer.

"Can you imagine not having Stephie to love? She's just an innocent child and surely not responsible for who her father is."

Mara had tears in her eyes again. Del continued, "Why don't you take a little time and think over what I've said. If you want me to, on Monday morning I'll call and set up an appointment at that place I told you about. I know they can help you, and I'll be with you so you don't have to go it alone."

Tears spilling down her cheeks, the girl reluctantly agreed. Del patted her arm and left her sitting at the table, while she herself went out into the healing garden to work with her hands and intercede with her heart.

47

The Day the Goose Dropped In

Later that day it seemed as if they were almost back into their normal routine. Del washed clothes and the two of them hung the shirts out on the clothesline, behind the windmill and well-hidden from the garden by a large Rose-of-Sharon bush. It soon became too hot to work outside, so Mara went to the computer to check her e-mail while Del prayed the Rosary in the living room. It wasn't long, however, before the girl came to talk. It seemed as if there was still a lot on her mind.

"I don't think it's fair," she complained, unaware that she was interrupting Del's quiet time. "Why should I have to suffer because of what someone else did to me?"

A good question, thought Del, opening her tired eyes which had just closed for a little rest. She sat up a little straighter to respond.

"I guess a lot of people would like to ask that question, child. There's a lot of unfairness in this world, like getting a terminal disease, being robbed, or having an accident that leaves you disabled. Or," Del ran a weary hand through her hair, "having your daughter killed by a drug addict."

She continued, "No, life isn't fair. We can't always control what's done to us, but we *can* decide how we're going to react to it. I really believe that God is with us through everything. With enough prayer, either the situation itself will change or we'll be given the grace necessary to handle it. Start to trust God now while you're young and it'll be easier when you're old like me!"

Then their conversation turned to one topic and another for the next couple hours. Del never did get her much-needed rest that day, but she was happy to notice that the girl seemed to feel a little freer to talk, now that the burden of keeping secrets had been lifted. There were even a few lighter moments that caused them both to smile. Quite a while later that afternoon, they realized that they needed to think about getting supper.

Del looked through her pantry and cupboards. It quickly dawned on her that, with all that had been going on that week, she had forgotten to pick up any groceries. So when she spied one of the jars of tomato sauce that she had put up the previous winter, she decided that spaghetti wouldn't take much time to make. But, although she got down on her hands and knees to pull everything off a shelf, she couldn't find any pasta.

"No problem," she finally declared. "We'll make some!"

Now Mara had never made pasta before. For all she knew, it had to come out of a box. However, she was willing to learn, so Del had her measure out the proper amount of flour into a large, wide stainless-steel bowl that she set on the kitchen table. Then she instructed Mara to get the eggs out of the refrigerator while she herself got a cup of water, and it was while they were thus engaged that the kitchen exploded.

Well, it didn't *actually* explode, but it certainly seemed that way. One moment it had been tranquil and calm in the kitchen, and the next there was a loud crash of glass breaking. Flour was flying everywhere amidst a great flapping of wings and general chaos. Both Del and Mara quickly spun around, their hearts leaping and their eyes popping, to see a huge Canada goose spreading its wings and attempting to jump out of the bowl of flour. Before they had a chance to do anything but gawk, the goose managed to tip the bowl and spill with it onto the floor, causing Mama Cat and her kittens to panic and scurry around, looking for a safe place to hide.

With cats scrambling around her feet, Del started to move cautiously towards the big grey bird. It tried to run, its long wings beating, and this stirred up the flour that had begun to settle. Big gusts of white flew up into the room like a cloud. There was blood running freely from gashes across the goose's chest, and the red drops were mixing in with the white all over the floor.

The goose seemed determined to go somewhere, anywhere, away from this craziness. Del quickly blocked the doorway into the living room, so there wasn't really any other place for it to go. But it kept trying, dodging in and out under the table, around and around the chairs. Mara, still holding the carton of eggs in her hand, watched with wide eyes and stayed out of the way. She clearly remembered Del's story about how hard geese could bite.

Finally, the panicky creature ran right past Del and she captured it by its long, black neck. It tried flapping its wings to get away, but the woman pinned those with her free hand and finally subdued the poor thing. She shouted at Mara to grab a towel and get it wet. They carefully wiped the blood from the bird's chest feathers so they could see how badly it was injured. Luckily, there didn't seem to be anything more than surface wounds. Del instructed the girl to smear on some antiseptic and then she awkwardly carted the bird to the back door where she released it into the garden. They watched the goose take fast running steps down the main path, until its long beating wings lifted its body from the ground and it flew off over the back line of trees.

Closing the door, Del walked back into the kitchen to survey the damage and stepped right in a pile of goose poop. As she looked down ruefully at the sole of her shoe, Mara started to snicker. Del glared at her and then noticed the condition of the kitchen. Flour had settled everywhere – on the stove, counters, chairs and table. There were drips of blood on the floor and glass shards mixed in with everything else. She groaned, shaking her head. Then she imagined how she herself must look, dusted in white like a floury ghost, and her face began to twitch.

The girl guffawed and Del let out a whoop, and they both laughed so hard they had to yank out chairs and drop into them. *That* caused the flour on the seats to fly up like a cloud. So, naturally, they chortled even more. Just at that moment the phone rang in the bedroom. Del, kicking off her shoes on the way, ran for it while trying to get herself under control.

Mara wiped away tears of laughter from her eyes, leaving streaks of gluey flour across her face. When Del came back, she could only point at the mess on Mara while cracking up again and holding her aching sides. It was quite some time before she regained enough sobriety to state that it had been Richard on the phone, calling to say that Ann's contractions had started again.

"He must have thought I was loony! I was gasping for air and trying to talk, and here he was, asking for prayers for Ann and the baby! Well!" Del took several deep breaths interspersed with a few last chuckles.

It took hours to clean up the disaster in the kitchen. While they swept, wiped and scrubbed, they discussed the improbability of a goose crashing through the window. Could it have thought it was coming to dinner?

"I only have goose for dinner on Christmas!" Del exclaimed, to a fresh round of giggles.

"Maybe it thought the big window was a lake to land on!" offered Mara.

"Or it saw its own reflection and thought it was another goose!"

On and on they went, laughing together and working side by side, until at last they were finished and both had taken showers. There was still one final task. Del went to her bedroom and brought back a large, flat sheet in a flowery print. With the girl's help, she stapled the edges of the sheet onto the window frame and stepped back to survey her work.

"Well, at least it'll keep the bugs out for now. I'll call my insurance company on Monday and arrange to have the glass replaced. Until then, it just won't be the same, looking at *those* flowers!"

Del scrambled some eggs for an easy dinner. As dusk set in, they were both so exhausted they decided to make an early night of it. Mara headed to her room and Del locked up the house and turned off all the lights. Then she sat at the kitchen table to pray quietly for a few moments in the stillness of twilight.

Outside, shadows were fading into darkness across the backyard and it was becoming increasingly difficult to see anything clearly. Even so, had there not been a sheet over the window, Del would have been sure to notice that there was someone in the garden.

48

Evil Enters the Garden

Sunday morning was one of those hazy, humid August days that makes one feel drained before even getting out of bed. The garden chores in the already-blazing sun were kept to a minimum. While she was watering the plants which really needed a drink, Del kept looking around her uneasily. She would have been hard pressed to explain the cause of her vague anxiety.

Maybe it's just this unbearable weather. It's like a wet blanket out here. I can hardly breathe. Finishing up quickly, she hurried into the cooler house. She let the girl sleep in as late as possible before awakening her and rushing off to noon Mass.

Driving into town, Del mentioned that it was her turn again to take Communion to shut-ins. She asked the girl if she would like to go to the Spencer farm after Mass to help Ann, and Mara readily agreed. They noticed Richard brought Sean and Abby with him this day to church. *To give their mom some peace and quiet, no doubt!* smiled Del to herself.

When Mass was over, Richard told Del that the doctor was insisting even more strongly that Ann stay in bed. By doing so, the contractions might stop and it would give the baby a little more time to grow. So he was delighted to have Mara come over to help with the dishes and laundry.

"We're a bit backed up on that stuff," he admitted sheepishly. Del laughed, knowing that was probably an understatement, and she intended to pitch in as well when she picked up Mara. She waved as they drove away, then walked through the church to where Father Mike was waiting with the Holy Eucharist.

Her Communion visits today were tinged with sadness because of the loss of her friend Esther. Her heart was heavy as she returned to church, put away the empty pyx and sank down before her Lord in the tabernacle. She had a lot to talk over with

God this day, pouring out all her ragged emotions from the week's events and asking for guidance along each step of the way. She spent a little extra time there in the presence of her Lord and King, just loving him and letting him love her.

All of a sudden the conviction hit her that she *must* go talk to Gerry, so she locked the doors after her and trotted down the street to his office. Gerry was the only full-time police officer in this small town and Del needed to find out if there was some legal recourse for Mara. *And I think it's about time I clear up any concerns about being held responsible for not reporting her as a runaway. Gerry is a grandfather himself and he'll be understanding about the situation.*

Del *did* feel much better after explaining everything to the officer. He told her to bring the girl in on Monday and they would figure out the best thing to do. Meanwhile, he'd try to find any information he could about a missing teen from the southwest part of Ohio. As Del left his office, she mopped her brow and sighed in relief. *Somehow things will work out.*

It was late in the afternoon when she arrived at the Spencer farm, and there she found mass confusion. Ann's water had just broken and contractions had started in earnest. Abby, all keyed up, was running around, while Richard was trying with no luck to get hold of his mother on the phone.

"I don't know where she is! She promised to stay home, in case I needed her to babysit in a hurry!"

"Just slow down. Don't worry," Del said in a maddeningly calm tone. "I'll take the kids home with me and keep phoning 'til I get her. Now call the hospital and go get your wife."

Richard did as suggested, disappearing up the stairs while Del tried unsuccessfully to get Abby to sit down and be quiet. Sean stayed out of the way of everyone, until he was told to get together everything that he and his sister needed to take to Grandma's house. Grateful to be doing something useful, he ran upstairs, nearly colliding with his father and mother walking carefully down.

Ann looked hot, tired and ready to have the baby *now*. Del shooed the two of them out the door, assuring them she'd pray for a safe delivery and a healthy baby. Then she gathered up the kids and all their stuff, and somehow got everyone and everything packed into the old boat. Even in the car, things didn't settle down, as Abby in her excitement was bouncing all over. If it hadn't been so chaotic, chances are that one of them might have seen the tire tracks veering off through the dusty roadside weeds and ending behind a heavy thicket. But they were distracted by the little girl's constant chatter, and the short drive to Windmill Gardens seemed the longest they had ever made.

As they pulled up to the house, Abby insisted that she was the person who needed to push the button to raise the garage door. Del responded mildly, "No, sweetie, we're going to leave the car right here in the driveway. I'll take you over to Grandma's as soon as I get in touch with her."

After getting out of the car, Del looked around and announced, "There's a storm on the way."

Surprised, Mara looked up at the cloudless blue sky. "How do you know that?"

The woman pointed to the trees. "Whenever you can see the bottom sides of the leaves reaching upwards, you can generally expect rain. Besides," she said, stretching painfully, "I can feel it in my joints."

They hurried to get the children out of the sun and into the house, where they set fans to circulate some air. When asked, Mara ran outside to bring in the wash from the clothesline, and returned with dry shirts in her arms.

"Have you seen my T-shirt?" she asked.

"Which one?"

"The one I had on when I came here."

Del thought a minute. The girl's shirt was rather distinctive, having a cartoon picture of a cat on its front. She was sure that she had hung it outside to dry yesterday.

"Wasn't it out there?" Del questioned.

"No."

The woman scratched her head. "That's strange. I know I hung it out on the line. Well," she continued, "occasionally a big old raccoon will get into my garden and take off with something. We'll probably find it eventually, stuffed into a tree hole somewhere in the woods."

Del turned back to the book she was reading to Sean and Abby, but the missing shirt played around in the back of her mind. *A raccoon? Climbing up a metal pole and pulling down that particular shirt? Seems hardly likely.* Yet Del had more immediate concerns with taking care of the children, and the incident with the shirt was set aside for the time being.

49

The Storm

Del had been right about the weather. Angry-looking dark clouds were rapidly building and covering the blue sky. A hot wind had picked up in the early evening, blowing the tops of the flowers in gusts. It didn't help relieve the oppressiveness of the humidity but simply added to it. Del had put together a cold supper for all of them, before finally getting an answer to her phone message left at the home of Richard's parents.

His brother called and assured Del that his mother was on her way home after visiting a sick relative, and that he himself would come right over to pick up the kids. However, by the time he got there it was well after eight o'clock, and he apologized for his lateness.

"Noticed the storm rollin' in and I had to batten the hatches before comin'," he explained. Although not as tall as Richard, he had the same wide friendly smile. "Then, just as I got back to the house, Richard called from the hospital. They barely made it there in time, seein' as how it was such a long drive to the city. Ann's had a fine baby boy, five pounds, fourteen ounces."

On hearing the news, Abby started jumping and prancing around again. Sean came over and tugged on his uncle's sleeve.

"Is Mom all right? What's his name gonna be?" he asked all in one breath.

"She's doin' well! And your new brother is Jacob Mark Spencer. Now both of you run along and get your stuff together. We have to get movin' before this storm hits!"

After the three of them had left, Del trotted out to her car to pull it into the garage. As the door lowered, she started to head back into the house. But she suddenly stopped. The back door of the garage, the one that led into the garden, was standing open. With a frown on her face, she pulled it shut.

174

Was the wind strong enough to blow open a door? Also, she was still troubled about the missing shirt, but tried to brush off her anxiety as just a feeling brought on by the approaching storm. Back in the kitchen, she and Mara straightened up the disarray from supper.

"At least it's not as bad as it was *last* night," Del said with a smile. Mara agreed that *had* been the biggest mess she'd ever seen. As they worked, they noticed it was growing obviously darker by the minute even though they could no longer see through the sheet-covered kitchen window. Distant rumblings of thunder were heard.

Del switched on lights in the house and locked the doors. She still couldn't put a finger on why she had that feeling of uneasiness in the pit of her stomach. *Maybe,* she pondered, *it's because summer storms always bring back memories of the last time I saw my brother. It was at that awful run-down apartment in Chicago. I had finally found him and was so happy to see him again. But he certainly wasn't happy to see me.*

Her heart heavy, Del remembered all his ranting and raving. She had become so frightened when he loomed over her, his eyes wild and his hands trembling, that she had dodged quickly around him and fled through the door. Down the decrepit old stairway she ran, out into the pounding rain of one of the worst storms she had ever seen.

These painful memories were part of her. However, Del was a woman of uncommon good sense who was not about to let the long-ago past have a bearing on what was happening now. She resolutely refocused on the present. Those odd things that had happened today were what she needed to deal with. She wasn't about to disregard her intuitions which were usually pretty accurate.

At last she made a decision. Telling the girl that she was going to make a phone call, she went to her bedroom and closed the door. *No use getting her upset over what may be nothing,* she thought. Her intent was to give Gerry a call and ask him to come and check out her yard and the surrounding area.

Mara grew tired of the magazine she had been leafing through and set it down next to her on the couch. It was likely she didn't give a second thought to Del making a phone call, which was probably to tell someone she knew about the Spencers' new baby. The girl saw a subdued flash of lightning through the taut

175

sheet covering the picture window and went into the back room to get a better look. The small window in the door, however, could give her no more than a snapshot of the panorama outside. She unlocked the door and stepped out, intending to stay by the house beneath the roof overhang to watch the jagged lightning cutting through black-clouded skies.

Just at that moment, though, Mama Cat suddenly saw her opportunity. She had been prowling about skittishly for the last hour or so, her tail twitching back and forth, as she felt the storm building in intensity. Like a panicky horse running back into a burning barn, it was just like an animal to go *into,* rather than *away from,* what it feared most. And so it was that Mama Cat, fearing the storm, saw the door open and ran out into exactly what was making her afraid.

Mara saw her streak out into the garden, but it was too late to stop her. The cat ran part way down the main path, then stopped and crouched down, meowing pitifully. Squinting, Mara could just barely make out the animal's white patches of fur against the dark ground. She said, "Here, kitty, kitty, kitty," as she had heard Del call the cat to her food every morning. But Mama was having none of it, staying immobilized in one place.

The girl sighed.

"Stupid cat," she muttered, then scanned the greenish-black overcast sky. Although thunder was rumbling almost constantly, the lightning seemed far away and rain had not yet begun to fall. So, concerned for the baby kittens who would be without their mother if anything happened to the cat, she started down the path towards Mama.

However, the terrified animal, hearing the approach of the girl, sprang up and ran even further away. Mara followed, calling over and over again, "Here, kitty, kitty, kitty." In the darkness she had to find her way along mostly by memory.

She finally caught up to Mama Cat at the far end of the garden, where the animal was attempting to climb the large tree. Speaking in a soothing voice, Mara came quietly up behind her and petted and scratched the cat behind the ears. In a moment, Mama had relaxed enough for the girl to pull her off the tree and cradle her in her arms. Still talking calmly and steadily, she turned to take the cat back to the house.

Meanwhile, Del was finishing her conversation with the police officer.

"I'll try to take a run out to your place," said Gerry. "Only problem is, this storm's coming on fast and I don't know if I can beat it. I also have to stop first at the McCormick's to settle a problem there. But I'll come as soon as I can."

Del thanked him and hung up. She had no way of knowing that he sat there for a few moments after their conversation ended, rubbing his grizzled chin and thinking. Gerry had known Del for a long time. In his opinion, she was not one to be afraid of shadows. If she was so uneasy as to give him a call late on a stormy Sunday evening, maybe there really *was* something going on. He suddenly changed the plans he had told her and left the office in a hurry, pulling on his rain gear as he went.

In the dark garden, Mara was stroking and talking to the cat as she felt her way along the wood-chipped path back to the house. Halfway there, she looked up to see a dark figure silhouetted against the light glowing through the sheet-covered window.

"Del?" she asked hesitantly, coming to a halt.

Except for the thunder which was continually growing louder, there was only silence. Mara's heart jumped and she could hear it pounding loudly inside her head. She kept staring at the figure but couldn't make out anything from the weak flashes of lightning, except for one thing – whoever it was, wasn't moving. Scared and trembling, she stood there rooted to the spot.

In a moment, she could hear shuffling on the wood chips as the figure began moving slowly toward her. Terrified, she took a step backward, then another. The cat leaped from her arms when she lost her balance stepping into one of the gardens, but she quickly recovered her footing and got back on the path. The figure was closer now and Mara, frightened beyond imagination, her breathing ragged, was poised to run. All of a sudden, a great bolt of lightning tore through the sky and lit up the person's face.

Mara screamed, and the man reached out an arm to grab her as she turned to flee. She dodged his grasp, but had barely a chance to get moving before he threw himself at her and knocked her to the ground. She struggled, screaming and kicking. However, his strong arms held on tightly as he dragged her to her feet.

Back in the house, Del had hung up the phone and was looking for Mara. The girl wasn't in any of the bedrooms nor the bathroom, and it wasn't until Del walked into the kitchen that she saw the back door standing open. Worried now, she wondered why in the world the girl would go outside with a storm fast approaching. Even though it wasn't yet raining, out of habit the woman slipped on her garden shoes before stepping out onto the patio.

She paused a moment to let her eyes adjust to the blackness outside. Just then lightning lit up the landscape with a bright flash, and she heard the girl scream and saw a dark, looming figure. Del hurried back into the house, where she rummaged through a closet for her husband's old hunting rifle. *There's no shells,* she thought wildly, *but maybe he won't realize that!*

Out in the garden, hidden by darkness, she moved quietly but sure-footed along the familiar main path where she could hear a struggle taking place. Taking shallow breaths, she crept closer and closer until she could see the back of a man who was attempting to hold on to the girl.

"Stop!" Del shouted against the rising wind, aiming the rifle and sighting along it like she knew what she was doing. "Stop! Let her go!"

The man turned quickly, bringing Mara around in front of him as if to use her for a shield. There they stood, frozen in time for a moment, the woman pointing the rifle at the man who was tightly grasping the struggling girl. Del, still unable to see his shadowed face, finally demanded boldly, "Who *are* you? And what do you want?"

He didn't answer, but the girl, trying desperately to pull her arms free, managed to gasp out in a terror-stricken voice, "Del! It's *Tom!*"

Tom?! How had he found the girl? But Del, even though she was quaking inside, kept the rifle aimed steadily and repeated, "Let her go!"

At that the man laughed, a harsh, raspy sound in the night.

"Now don't make me do anything," he said roughly, "that you'll regret."

With the girl clutched tightly to him, he began moving slowly to his left through the garden, feeling his way along and demolishing plants as he dragged the girl with him.

Thunder rolled more loudly and lightning split the sky as Del followed. With the rifle pointed and a desperate prayer on her lips, she stayed close but out of reach. The man kept edging his way backwards and sideways in a semi-circle around her, always holding the girl in front of him. Once he nearly lost his balance when he bumped into and knocked over the tomato cages, but he caught himself and re-tightened his hold on Mara.

Where is he going? thought Del, keeping him in her sights. *If he wants to get out, the gate's on the other side!* The man was almost to the windmill. *Maybe he's heading for the garage.*

At that thought Del nearly panicked, remembering all the tools in there that could be used as weapons. And here she was with only an unloaded rifle!

Now he was under the windmill and moving toward the garage. But he didn't get very far because, unexpectedly, Mara got one arm free and grabbed the leg of the windmill. He tried pulling on her but his grip must have loosened. All of a sudden she twisted her body sideways, broke away from him and ran off. Before Del even had a chance to react, the man lunged at the woman and grabbed the barrel of the rifle. Trying to point it skyward, he quickly pulled Del closer to him. As he attempted to yank the gun from her grasp, he locked his other hand onto the steel windmill, and that's when it happened.

In that split second Del realized what was coming. Feeling her hair stand on end and her skin tingle, she let go of the rifle at the same instant that thunder crashed and a bolt of lightning struck the windmill. She felt a tremendous shock of power surge through her, and instantaneous mind-numbing pain. Large drops of rain spattered her face as she began to crumple to the ground and lose consciousness. The last thing she heard was the girl screaming and the sound of a police siren in the distance.

50

Resurrection

The hospital room was quiet except for the soft beeping of a machine next to the bed. The draperies were pulled to keep out the hot afternoon sun, and the room lights were dimmed so the woman in the bed could sleep. Next to her sat a teenage girl keeping a vigil. Her hair was pulled back from her thin, pale face into a haphazard ponytail, and an occasional tear threatened to escape from her red-rimmed eyes. The girl had talked to the doctor earlier, and he told her that Del was lucky to be alive.

"It may have been those rubber soles on her shoes that protected her, or the fact that the ground was still dry. Who knows?"

Since the woman had briefly regained consciousness that morning and the doctor had spoken to her, he thought it would be all right if the girl stayed in the room until Del woke up again. So Mara sat waiting, with plenty of time to think. She looked at the woman's bandaged hands and singed hair, and maybe she wondered what would cause Del, who had known her less than two months, to put her own life on the line for her. The girl continued to watch the woman closely to make sure she didn't stop breathing or anything like that, even though there were monitors hooked up for that sort of thing.

From between the window draperies where they didn't close completely, a shaft of light stole through and lay as a gold stripe across Del's feet. As the afternoon passed, Mara watched the bright line creep slowly up the woman's blanketed legs. By the time it had reached the midpoint of the bed, there was a short crosspiece to it. Puzzled, the girl leaned across Del and was able to block out the light by passing her hand back and forth. But, try as she might, she couldn't see where anything more than a single line of sunshine was coming through the narrow opening in the drapes.

Sitting back again, she kept her eye on the cross of light moving slowly upwards on the bed as the sun sank lower in the sky. Late in the afternoon, the cross reached the region of Del's heart. But at that point the girl forgot about it, because just then the woman woke up.

Del turned her head and saw Mara. She smiled at her.

"How long have you been sitting here?" she asked faintly.

"All afternoon," replied the girl, starting to sniffle.

"Don't worry, child. The doctor told me I'm going to be just fine. My left eardrum is perforated but it'll heal, and so will my hands. And my hair will grow back. Maybe," Del continued with some of that old twinkle in her eye, "if I'm lucky it'll grow in black instead of grey!"

Mara smiled a little through the threatening tears, but the next thought brought a soft wail with it.

"But...but Del! The garden! It's ruined! What with the pouring rain and the police and ambulance people trampling through it...oh, Del, it's a real mess!" Tears spilled down her face as the girl thought about the once-beautiful garden and how it had helped bring a measure of peace into her life.

But Del looked at it another way.

"Child," she began, "it's just a garden, something that God has given us to make life a little more enjoyable." She was thoughtful a moment. "I had a friend once who said that *things* are to be used, and *people* are to be cherished. Not the other way around. How right she was! The garden isn't as important as *you* are. Besides, it can be fixed up again. I'm just glad to see that you're all right."

Mara nodded, then Del asked her, "What happened to Tom?"

The girl lowered her head before answering.

"He's dead. From the lightning."

Del didn't say anything. The only sound in the room was from their breathing and the machine nearby. After a long time, without looking up, the girl spoke softly.

"I know you said how important it is to forgive someone who's hurt you. But, Del," she glanced up, her eyes shimmering, "I don't know if I can ever forgive that man."

Del took a moment before answering.

"I understand what you're saying. Give yourself time. Maybe a lot of time. And you'll only be able to do it with God's

181

help. But always remember that unforgiveness, and all those other negative things that we hold onto, stop up our conduit and take away our peace and joy."

She sighed and continued, "Then we're of little use to anyone, especially God. He can work in powerful ways inside of us, and he can work in other people's lives *through* us, if we just keep that conduit clear."

Then she asked, "Is this the same hospital that Ann's in?" The girl nodded, saying that Gerry had brought her in after lunch, and that she had been able to visit Ann and little Jacob for a few minutes before coming to Del's room.

"And this morning Gerry called my mother and told her everything. Then I talked to her for a long time and we both cried a lot. It turns out that my mother's been afraid of him, too, for a long time." Mara took a deep, shaky breath.

"He was able to find me because when he got the bill from the credit card I took, he found out the town where I bought all that stuff. And Pete's mom discovered my e-mail where I said I was in Michigan. She told my mother, who wanted to call the police. But Tom said no, that he'd go and find me. I think he wanted to make sure I wasn't going to tell on him."

The girl was getting more upset.

"I was so stupid! I had mentioned the beautiful garden and the windmill. All he had to do was ask around when he got to the general area, because a lot of people know about Windmill Gardens. This is all my fault!"

Del said softly, "Child, don't take the blame for other people's actions. You can't control what others decide to do, only what *you* do. Speaking of that, what are you going to do about the baby? *Your* baby."

Mara shook her head, taking awhile to answer.

"I don't know yet. Gerry showed me a picture of one of his grandchildren. Said she was adopted and 'much loved by her family,' as he put it. He said maybe I should consider that option."

Mara pulled a tissue from the box on the bedside table and dried her eyes and face.

"Mom told him that she had her hands full right now, what with Tom's death and all, so it was okay with her if you take me to see a counselor. In any case, my mother said she'd help me, whatever I decide. She wanted to drive up next weekend to get me, but I asked her if I could stay with you 'til school starts. You know, to help with the garden while your hands heal."

She added anxiously, "That's all right, isn't it?" and Del smiled, assuring her that that would be wonderful.

Mara went on, "I was thinking that when Richard comes tonight to visit Ann, I'll have him drop me off at your house and I'll start cleaning up the garden."

The girl was quiet for a moment before asking a final question.

"Del, do you think that God killed Tom?"

Del thought a minute before answering in a tired voice.

"Child, I don't know. But I don't think God kills anyone. There's nothing we can ever do, no matter how bad, that makes God stop loving us. It's *we* who stop loving him. He gives us free choice, and we can choose to do wrong if we want to. Tom died because he *chose* to be there in the garden with evil in his heart, just when that lightning was about to strike."

Mara didn't say anything else, but got to her feet and did something that was very unlike her. She leaned over and kissed Del on the forehead, then she hurried out of the room. Smiling a little, Del watched her leave before closing her eyes and turning her thoughts once again towards her Lord.

She prayed in thanksgiving for Richard and Ann's new baby. She prayed for the girl and her unborn child, that God would watch over them both, keep them safe and pour out his blessings on them. She prayed for Mara's mother, so she might find peace in her own life and be a strong support for her daughter.

Finally, just before drifting off to sleep again, she thought about the man who had been the cause of so much pain to others. And Del, being Del, prayed also for Tom, that God would have mercy on his soul.

Endnotes

For further reading:
Dives in Misericordia (Rich in Mercy), encyclical of Pope John Paul II, written November, 1980.

    www.vatican.va/holy_father/john_paul_ii/encyclicals

Divine Mercy in My Soul, diary of St. Maria Faustina Kowalska, Marian Press, Stockbridge, MA, 1987.

    www.marian.org/divinemercy/devotion.html

Chapter 11 – "Wilding"

For more information on wild plants:
Edible Wild Plants, Lee Allen Peterson, Houghten Mifflin Company, New York, 1977.

Identifying and Harvesting Edible and Medicinal Plants, Steve Brill with Evelyn Dean, William Morrow and Company, New York, 1994.

Note: Do not gather plants in the wild unless you are experienced at identifying edible species. There are many poisonous look-alikes.

Chapter 17 – "Sunday"

Padre Pio, ordained in 1910, was a humble Italian friar who was given many extraordinary gifts by God. However, he was best known for the long hours he spent hearing confessions and for his passionate love for Jesus in the Holy Eucharist. For more information on his life, go to www.ewtn.com/padrepio.

Chapter 20 – "A Cherry Interesting Conversation"

Heaven:
    1Corinthians 2:9: "It is written, 'Eye has not seen, nor ear heard, nor has it entered the human heart, what God has prepared for those who love him.'"

Love of others:
    1John 4:10-11: "In this is love, not that we loved God but that he loved us and sent his Son to be the expiation for our sins. Beloved, if God so loved us, we also ought to love one another."
    1John 4:20-21: "If anyone says, 'I love God,' and hates his brother, he is a liar; for he who does not love his brother whom he has seen, cannot love God whom he has not seen. And this commandment we have from him, that he who loves God should love his brother also."

Chapter 23 – "Del's Prayer"

Satan, the Deceiver:

John 8:44: "He [Satan] was a murderer from the beginning, and has nothing to do with the truth, because there is no truth in him. When he lies, he speaks according to his own nature, for he is a liar and the father of lies."

Praying in the presence of the Lord:

Lamentations 2:19b: "Pour out your heart like water before the presence of the Lord!"

Chapter 25 – "Back to Nature"

For those who suffer physical, emotional or behavioral problems, sometimes a diet free of synthetic additives can help. For more information, contact:

The Feingold Association of the U.S.
127 E. Main Street #106
Riverhead, NY 11901
1-800-321-3287   www.feingold.org

Chapter 26 – "The Rosary"

The Bible tells us to pray always:

1Thessalonians 5:17: "Pray without ceasing."

Our Father:

Matthew 6:9: "Pray then like this: Our Father who art in heaven, hallowed be thy name. Thy kingdom come, thy will be done, on earth as it is in heaven. Give us this day our daily bread; and forgive us our debts, as we have forgiven our debtors; and lead us not into temptation, but deliver us from evil."

Hail Mary:

Luke 1:28: "And he [Gabriel] came to her and said, 'Hail, full of grace, the Lord is with you.'"

Luke 1:42: "And she [Elizabeth] exclaimed with a loud cry, 'Blessed are you among women, and blessed is the fruit of your womb!'"

Chapter 27- "Forgive Us Our Trespasses"

It sounds as if God won't forgive us if we don't forgive others:

Matthew 6:14: "[Jesus said,] 'For if you forgive men their trespasses, your heavenly Father will forgive you; but if you do not forgive men their trespasses, neither will your Father forgive your trespasses.'"

Kateri Tekakwitha was born in 1656 of a Christian Algonquin mother and a non-Christian Mohawk father. She was orphaned at a young age by a smallpox epidemic which also left her scarred and partially blind. Converted and baptized by a Jesuit missionary, she was held in contempt and derision by her people. She consecrated herself entirely to Jesus and spent the rest of her life in prayer, penance and care of the sick and aged. She died at the age of 24, and was beatified by the Church in 1980. For more information, go to www.kateritekakwitha.org.

Chapter 30 – "Mercy and Forgiveness"

Confess your sins to another:
James 5:16: "Therefore confess your sins to one another, and pray for one another, that you may be healed."

Forgiving or retaining sins:
John 20:21-23: "Jesus said to them again, 'Peace be with you. As the Father has sent me, even so I send you.' And when he had said this, he breathed on them, and said to them, 'Receive the Holy Spirit. If you forgive the sins of any, they are forgiven; if you retain the sins of any, they are retained.'"

For more information on the Catholic Faith:
Catechism of the Catholic Church, 1997, Libreria Editrice Vaticana (available at bookstores or online at www.vatican.va)
www.catholicoutlook.com
www.internetpadre.org
www.jimmyakin.com

Chapter 32 – "Fourth of July"

Putting God first in everything:
Matthew 6:33: "But seek first the kingdom of God and his righteousness, and all these things will be yours as well."

Chapter 35 – "Another Mother"

Mary as our mother:
John 19:27a: "Then he said to the disciple, 'Behold, your mother!'"

Those in heaven are alive:
Mark 12:27a: "He is not the God of the dead, but of the living."
John 11:25-26: "Jesus said to her, 'I am the resurrection and the life; he who believes in me, though he die, yet shall he live, and whoever lives and believes in me shall never die. Do you believe this?'"

A person can be friends with God:

John 15:14-15a: "[Jesus said,] 'You are my friends if you do what I command you. No longer do I call you servants, for a servant does not know what his master is doing; but I have called you friends...'"

Jesus was like us:

Hebrews 4:15: "For we have not a high priest who is unable to sympathize with our weaknesses, but one who in every respect has been tempted as we are, yet without sinning."

Chapter 37 – "Communion"

This is my body; this is my blood:

Matthew 26:26-28: "Now as they were eating, Jesus took bread, and blessed, and broke it, and gave it to the disciples and said, 'Take, eat; this is my body.' And he took a cup, and when he had given thanks he gave it to them, saying, 'Drink of it, all of you; for this is my blood of the covenant, which is poured out for many for the forgiveness of sins.'" (See also Luke 22:19-20 and Mark 14:22-24)

Jesus the bread from heaven:

John 6:51: "I am the living bread which came down from heaven; if anyone eats of this bread, he will live forever; and the bread which I shall give for the life of the world is my flesh."

Jews were quarreling among themselves:

John 6:52-56: "The Jews disputed among themselves, saying, 'How can this man give us his flesh to eat?' So Jesus said to them, 'Truly, truly, I say to you, unless you eat the flesh of the Son of man and drink his blood, you have no life in you; he who eats my flesh and drinks my blood has eternal life, and I will raise him up at the last day. For my flesh is food indeed, and my blood is drink indeed. He who eats my flesh and drinks my blood abides in me, and I in him.'"

Jesus' disciples didn't get it:

John 6: 66: "After this many of his disciples drew back and no longer went about with him."

Why would Jesus give us himself as food and drink?:

"When God desired to give a food to our soul to sustain it in the pilgrimage of life, he looked upon creation and found nothing that was worthy of it. Then he turned again to himself, and resolved to give himself...O my soul, how great you are, since only God can satisfy you! The food of the soul is the body and blood of a God. O glorious food! The soul can feed only on God; only God can suffice it; only God can fill it; only God can satiate its hunger…My God, how can it be that Christians actually remain so long without giving this food to their poor souls? They leave them to die of want." – St. John Mary Vianney

Chapter 38 – "From Peace to Peaches"

Jesus, are you really here?:
Matthew 28:20b: "Lo, I am with you always, to the close of the age."

Chapter 46 – "Confessions"

Mother Teresa, the founder of the Missionaries of Charities religious order, was known all over the world for her passionate commitment to the poor and unloved. In them she saw Jesus "in his most distressing disguise." She often spoke out against abortion, saying that it was the biggest destroyer of peace in the world, for if a mother can kill her own child, what's to stop you and me from killing each other? She died in 1997at the age of 87 in Calcutta, India.

Psalm of the day:
Psalm 25

Chapter 50 – "Resurrection"

I don't think God kills anyone:
Ezekiel 33:11: "Say to them, As I live, says the Lord God, I have no pleasure in the death of the wicked, but that the wicked turn from his way and live…"

For help with an unplanned pregnancy:
The Nurturing Network at 1-800-TNN-4MOM
www.nurturingnetwork.org
or Birthright at 1-800-550-4900
www.birthright.org

Hurting after an abortion?
Call 1-877-HOPE-4-ME
www.rachelsvineyard.org

Book Discussion/Reflection Questions

1. Del told Richard that he needed to have a "plan for prayer" or he wouldn't pray. Do you think this statement is true, and what would such a plan entail?

> Do you have a plan for your own prayer life?
> If not, how could you go about developing one?
> If so, how has your plan changed over time?

2. St. Mary Faustina Kowalska has given the world the "Divine Mercy" message (as contained in her diary *Divine Mercy in My Soul*) that God's mercy and forgiveness is freely given to anyone who comes to him with a repentant heart and asks for it. Del experienced that mercy of God in a profound way in her life. What way, big or small, have you been touched in your life by Divine Mercy?

3. Both Del and Mara ran away from their respective homes after traumatic events in their lives. Can "running away from problems" be a legitimate response to overwhelming difficulties? How else might they have dealt with their problems?

4. Mara makes several attempts to pray, but other thoughts crowd in and lead her to thinking about other things. Is there anyone you can think of in our present day who might have a distraction-free prayer life? Anyone in the past? How do *you* handle distractions at prayer?

5. Del explains to the girl how we can all be "conduits" for God's love and grace to flow through us into the lives of others. What kinds of things in our own lives "stop up" that conduit so that God's blessings can't flow through? Have you ever thought about asking God prayerfully what might be stopping up your conduit?

6. At the end of the story, Mara clearly has some important decisions to make. She might decide to go ahead and have an abortion anyway, or she might decide to give birth and raise the child herself or place the child in a loving, adoptive home. How do you think each of these decisions will affect her – physically, mentally and emotionally? From which decision do you think she will experience the greatest spiritual growth?